Seventh Place

Also by Kate Lattey

PONY JUMPERS

DARE TO DREAM

CLEARWATER BAY

For more information, visit nzponywriter.com

Email nzponywriter@gmail.com and sign up to my mailing list for exclusive previews, new releases, giveaways and more!

Pony Jumpers

#7

SEVENTH PLACE

Kate Lattey

ISBN-13: 978-1539902164
ISBN-10: 1539902161

– ♥ –

Love means attention,
which means looking after the things we love.
We call this stable management.

George Morris

– ♥ –

1

DOWN SOUTH

The island appeared out of the mist ahead of us, shimmering into existence as the large ferry motored across the Cook Strait. I leaned against the railing, the wind whipping my long blonde hair around my face, and stared out at the approaching South Island. I usually enjoyed this trip, but this year, for the first time, I'd begged Dad to skip the National Championships altogether and just let us stay at home.

He'd said no, of course. None of my arguments – that my top ponies Buck and Skip were already qualified for Pony of the Year so we didn't need the extra points; that I'd won Nationals last year and so had nothing left to prove; that my young pony Forbes didn't like long journeys or extended periods away from home and was unlikely to go well – had held weight. Dad had had answers for everything – yes the ponies were qualified, but they weren't at the top of the national table, so could always use more points; that I'd won it on Buck last year but not on Skip, and nobody had ever won it back to back, so another win would be impressive either way; and that Forbes had to get used to the travel sometime and he might as well start now.

And so here I was, with my father and, in a situation that was becoming increasingly commonplace, without my mother. She'd stopped coming to shows a few weeks ago, preferring to stay home and work while Dad and I travelled. A skilled interior decorator, Mum had only worked occasionally while I was growing up, taking on jobs that she liked and turning down anything she didn't feel particularly inspired by. But lately she'd decided to resurrect her business, and had started picking up contracts left, right and centre, and working every hour of the day. She'd moved into the home office, and when she wasn't shut up in there, she was out looking at fabric samples and paint swatches, trawling around furniture stores and hunting down light fittings that would add just the right touch to someone's room. She'd lost almost all interest in the ponies and my riding career, listening idly whenever Dad and I discussed them, but no longer contributing anything to the conversation. It was unsettling, because she used to be so invested in my riding that I could hardly turn around without her buying me new clothes or checking the national leader boards to see exactly what position I was sitting in.

But while it was unsettling for me, it was mindboggling for my father. If she could've picked one thing that would irritate him beyond all others, that was it. So he'd upped his game in response, taking more of an interest than ever before, coming down to the arena every evening when I was schooling and giving me pointers, offering to move jumps and poles around for me, and generally making a nuisance of himself. But I knew why he was doing it, so I didn't complain. I nodded, and smiled, and did as I was told.

As always.

My parents have never had a particularly affectionate relationship – that's just who they are. Hugs are hard to come by in our house, and feelings rarely discussed. But I'd never doubted that they loved each other until a few weeks ago, when my brother Pete had briefly returned from his exile in South Africa and tried to convince Mum to go back with him. She'd almost done it. Had almost left New Zealand, and had almost left my father. Had almost dragged me along with her, until she'd changed her mind at the last minute, much to my relief. I'd naïvely assumed that everything would go back to normal after that. But I should've known better. Nothing was ever normal in my house.

"There you are."

I turned my head and saw my father striding towards me, tall and upright, always looking like he's in a hurry to get somewhere more important. He stopped next to me and leaned one hand on the boat railing. His wedding ring glinted in the sunlight, and I wondered if they would get a divorce. It certainly wasn't outside of the realm of possibility, although it gave me a cold feeling to even consider it. I wasn't sure I could handle that much change.

"I told you I was coming up here," I reminded him, but he wasn't really listening.

"I've just been talking to the Campbells," he told me. "They've got a horse for sale that might suit you."

This again. "I don't want another horse."

"Now hear me out," he insisted, ignoring my objection as always. "It's a very well-bred jumper they imported from Australia last year for Grace, but it's a bit much for her to handle, apparently." *No kidding.* I didn't know the horse, but Grace Campbell was only about twelve years old and barely managing to get her super-reliable pony Summertime going consistently around the Pony Grand Prix circuit as it was. "Nothing that would trouble you, they assure me, just a bit spirited for her. Very talented though. It's won metre-forties over in Oz, and they say it's a super Young Rider prospect." He paused for a moment, then carried on. "Well, what do you think?"

I shrugged. "Why doesn't Connor ride it, if it's that good?"

"Too small for him. She's only fifteen-two, and slender-built."

I nodded. Connor was only a couple of years older than me, but he was over six feet tall. His long legs wrapped around a little 15.2hh mare would be laughable.

"What's her name?" I asked curiously, wondering if I'd seen the horse on the circuit. As much as I insisted to my father that I didn't

9

need a fourth mount, there were a few that I wouldn't necessarily have turned away.

"Small Talk," he told me. "It's not been out much. They've kept it at home and tried to get it going with Grace, but it's not working out, so they've brought it to Nationals to do the metre-twenty Champ. Got a friend riding it, apparently. Didn't say who."

I nodded again, and looked out over the sparkling blue water. "Right."

"I'll let them know we're interested then."

I turned my head and frowned at him. "I didn't say that. Dad, we've been over this. I've got three ponies already in work and school starts again in a few days. I don't have time to work four during the term."

"And I told you that I'd get you some help."

"I don't *want* help," I reminded him. "I can do it myself. I want to do it myself."

Dad sucked in a breath, clearly trying to school himself to patience. I looked away from his angry eyes and out across the blue ocean that rippled around us. Someone on the top deck shouted as a pair of bottlenose dolphins leapt out of the water, curving gracefully through the air, then diving back into the depths.

I envied them their freedom.

"We've talked about this."

"No, *you've* talked about this." I wasn't sure where the courage to talk back to him was coming from, but I embraced it. It wasn't something I did often, but something in the open sea air was giving me a stronger sense of self. "I've been sitting there, but you've been the one making decisions."

"You've only got a season and a half left on ponies," Dad said resolutely, as though by repeating himself yet again he could somehow change my mind. "And Buck's starting to feel his age."

I clenched my jaw, staring out across the water and willing the dolphins to come back. I didn't want to think about Buck. At eighteen years old and with a long career behind him, his joints were starting to wear down. We babied him along as much as possible, cosseting him with massage blankets and joint formulas, but nothing could reverse the process of time.

"He might not be a contender next season," Dad said, pressing down on that wound. "Could be we have to retire him after Pony of the Year. And then you'd be down to two, and it only makes sense to get a horse instead of another pony, so you can get started in the Young Riders."

"Might as well just retire him now," I snapped. "Might as well retire Skip too, he's fifteen, must be getting past it."

"Watch your tone," Dad warned me. "Just take a look at the horse, all right? Watch it go, see what you think. If you're not interested, then you're not. But they want it sold before winter, and the price is right."

He walked off as I continued to watch the Marlborough Sounds slide ever closer. I wanted to see out my pony years successfully, but I wasn't sure I even wanted to compete beyond that. Maybe I didn't need a horse. Maybe I'd just give up. Retire the older ponies, sell Forbes. Have a life outside of horses.

I wondered what that would even look like. I couldn't imagine it, because I'd never had one.

I turned my head away from the approaching shore, staring back out across the open water, but the dolphins never reappeared.

My three ponies cropped the grass greedily, stuffing their faces with it as though they hadn't eaten since we left Napier. The sun was going down, and it turned cold quickly in the South Island, even in summer. I shivered as a cool breeze whisked past, making Forbes's short mane stand on end. I zipped my puffa jacket up to my chin and flexed my cold fingers on the three lead ropes, watching the ponies munch. We'd finally arrived at McLeans Island an hour or so ago, and I had taken the ponies straight out to stretch their legs before letting them graze under the setting sun.

The show jumping rings were all set up, and Dad had managed to park reasonably close to Ring One, where the premier competitions would be starting tomorrow. Three classes over three days counted towards the overall championship, and consistency was key. The scoring was so complex that I never bothered to work it out, but Dad always did. He'd study the scoreboard every evening, working out exactly how many faults I had in hand, if any. Last year it'd been tight, but I'd managed to scrape the win.

I looked around at the venue, wishing I wasn't alone. No-one else in my small group of friends had made it all the way down to Nationals this year, which was just another reason that I hadn't wanted to come. But it wasn't a reason that Dad considered good enough to miss what was, outside of Pony of the Year, the biggest prize in New Zealand pony show jumping. So here we were, just me, my father and my ponies, for the next three days.

Buck's muzzle nudged the side of my boot as he sought out the patch of clover under my foot. He was such a good pony, and had been a far better pony for me than I'd deserved. I shifted my foot, giving him access to the coveted patch of grass. I owed it to him to make his life as easy as possible in his old age.

"At least Dad's not trying to sell you," I told the dark bay gelding. "He knows we're going to have to retire you ourselves. You'll like that, won't you? Getting to hang out in the paddock all day, not having to travel and compete anymore?" Buck blew out through his large nostrils as he ate, and I scratched his ears around his leather halter. "Soon, buddy. Only a couple more shows to finish out the season, and we'll see where we go from there."

Forbes lifted his head then, and Skip followed suit, both of them staring at something over my shoulder. I turned to see a big chestnut horse trotting in our direction with two other horses, one being ponied off each side. I recognised the rider at once, and felt my pulse quicken as he approached.

Connor Campbell. He rode well, as always, keeping his big chestnut Tiberius Rex under easy control. A steel grey with a white tail trotted on one side of him, and a pretty little bay on the other. I sized her up as they came closer. Fifteen-two would be about right. Slender, well-bred. This must be the horse that Dad had been going on about, and despite myself, I liked the look of her.

Connor noticed me, and to my surprise, he brought his horses closer, reining them in only a few metres away from where my ponies were grazing. Satisfied that he wasn't going to be trampled, Skip went back to eating, but Forbes was still paying keen attention to Connor's horses.

"Hey there."

I looked up at Connor, squinting into the setting sun behind him. "Hi."

I couldn't keep the wariness out of my tone, but for good reason. Connor hadn't exactly been friendly to me in the past, alternating between ignoring me and being outright mean, but he was being congenial enough right now. I guess that's what happened when your father approached people with an open chequebook. I knew that if I decided I wanted a horse badly enough, Dad would make it happen – whatever the price.

Connor shifted in the saddle and looked down at me. "Heard you were interested in one of our nags."

I shrugged coolly. "Dad mentioned something about it." Unable to stand the sunstrike any longer, I looked aside, and my eyes fell on the bay mare. "This one, is it?"

"Yeah. Get over, Rex." Connor shifted his weight, and the big chestnut stepped sideways, shading the sun from my eyes. "Better?"

I nodded. "Thanks." I studied the mare. She had good

conformation, slender but strong, with well-developed hindquarters and a sloping shoulder and graceful neck. "Nice-looking horse."

"If she was a couple hands bigger, she wouldn't be going anywhere. But she's far too small for me, and too much for Gracie."

As he spoke, the bay mare turned her head and whinnied, straining against the lead rope as a dark bay pony trotted past, its legs encased in fluffy pink paddock boots.

"Shut up, you egg," Connor told her, tugging on the lead rope, but the mare ignored his remonstrance and shifted her hindquarters into Rex as she tried to watch the pony circling behind her. The pony was a nice mover with smooth paces, and although it was being ridden in draw reins, they were loose enough to be barely having an effect. The rider sat well, with steady hands and low heels, and as she circled back in our direction, I recognised Connor's little sister in the saddle.

"Summer's looking good."

Connor glanced over his shoulder idly at Grace. "Be looking better without all that pink crap on her," he said, referring not only to the pony's hot pink boots but also her matching saddleblanket and Grace's pink puffa vest, which had some kind of sparkly diamante pattern on the back and a faux fur-lined hood.

"At least she's not chestnut," I told him. "Then it'd clash as well."

He rolled his eyes. "Yeah, guess we should be grateful for that," he agreed. "How're your lot going?"

"Um, okay." I was still a little flummoxed by the fact that I was standing here, having a perfectly friendly conversation with someone I'd spent the last year or so avoiding like the plague, and not without good reason. I was still wary, but it was nice to have someone to talk to. I lowered my guard slightly, and looked at the mare again. "So what's her name?"

"Star."

I frowned, looking at the mare's narrow blaze. "Interesting choice, since she doesn't have one."

"It's because she *is* one," Connor grinned. "Trust me, wait 'til you see her jump. Got springs in her legs, this horse. Like I said, if I could put it on stilts…" He shook his head in disappointment as Star whinnied loudly at Summer, who responded in a muffled sort of way. "She's only seven, got years left in her too." His eye scanned over Buck and Skip, and I knew he was well aware of their more advanced years.

"Why not just keep her then, let Grace grow into her?"

"Because it'll be years before she's up for it," he replied. "Waste of a good horse. Mum wants to, she's convinced Grace's overdue for a growth spurt, and that the moment we sell Star, Gracie'll shoot up like a beanstalk, but I'm not holding my breath. And Dad wants her gone, says she's a waste of space if neither of us are competing her."

"How does Grace feel about it?"

He shrugged. "Couldn't care less. She doesn't like Star anyway, reckons she's too hard to ride. She's looking for another Grand Prix pony instead, so keep your eyes open for something that a midget could ride."

I couldn't help grinning at that, and he winked down at me. *Damn.* There was no denying that Connor was attractive, with his dark eyes, slanting eyebrows, and high, carved cheekbones. *Don't even go there,* I told myself. *Dangerous territory.* Connor was one of a meagre handful of straight young men on the show jumping circuit, and hands-down the best-looking – a fact that he exploited on a regular basis. But I had no ambition to be his latest conquest.

"So who's riding Star this weekend?" I asked, trying to focus on the mare.

"Anna Harcourt," he said casually, and my heart sank. Another person who had it in for me. Unlike Connor, I couldn't imagine Anna changing her spots overnight. Boys didn't seem to hold grudges the way that girls did, but Anna had been front and centre of more than a few unpleasant incidents that I'd been on the receiving end of. I was pretty sure she was still in possession of the stud girth that had disappeared out of our truck here last year, but I'd never had any evidence to back up my suspicion that she was the one who'd taken it. Just a very solid hunch.

"Well, I guess we'll watch her jump tomorrow and see what we think," I told Connor, trying to sound noncommittal. *You don't need another horse*, I reminded myself. *Not even one as pretty as that.*

"Yeah, all right. She's on right after your first round, in Ring One. Your dad said you'd come try her sometime in the arvo, after the pony classes are done."

"Did he just?"

Connor smiled, and my heart fluttered slightly, defying what my head knew. *Bad idea,* I reminded it again. I knew that this was his game, that he was a player, and spent more time at shows trying to pick up girls than riding, but that didn't mean I couldn't look. There was no way in hell he was going to try to pick me up, anyway. He was only being friendly because he thought I might buy Star. Except that we'd now had that discussion, and he still hadn't ridden away. Instead he shifted his weight and loosened his reins, looking critically down at my ponies.

"I like Skybeau with a hogged mane."

I frowned, wondering what he meant by that. Skip's mane had been hacked off maliciously by another competitor a few weeks ago, and although I was currently keeping it tidy with clippers, I couldn't wait to let it grow back out again over winter.

"I don't," I said honestly.

Connor shrugged, then looked over his shoulder at his sister, who was still trotting around in circles. "Summer'll be too tired to jump tomorrow at this rate," he muttered. "Oi, Gracie! Give it a rest, would you?"

Grace didn't turn her head at his shout, but she did bring her pony back to a walk and give her a long rein. Summertime stretched her neck out willingly, and Grace patted her with a small hand. I wondered which pony they'd end up buying for her once Star was sold. Summer was no spring chicken herself.

"How old is she now?" I asked as Grace rode towards us, her short legs only a few inches below the flaps of the jumping saddle.

"Thirteen. Fourteen in April. Just short for your age, eh Gracie?" Connor replied, misunderstanding my question.

Grace had reached us now and halted her pony next to Star, frowning at her brother. "What?"

"You're a midget."

"Shut up." Star was nickering frantically at Summer, and straining at her lead in an attempt to touch the other mare. Connor yanked on the rope, jerking Star's head around and making me wince.

"Only flaw it's got," Connor said as he noticed me watching Star. "Bit clingy, but she's actually getting better, believe it or not. And she's only like this with mares. Couldn't care less about these two guys," he explained, motioning at the horse he was sitting on and the young grey, who had his eyes half-closed and was dozing quietly, resting a hind leg. "Reckon she's not into boys." He cocked an eyebrow suggestively as he looked at me, and I flushed.

"More fool her," I told him, and his grin widened.

"Too right."

Grace was still sitting silently and watching us, fiddling with a lock of Summer's mane. Forbes tugged at his lead rope, seeking out a more delicious patch of grass just to his right, and I brought him back into line as Connor gathered up his reins at last.

"Well, we better keep moving. See ya later, Susannah."

"Okay. See you."

They turned back towards the yards, Grace riding alongside her brother as he chatted to her while effortlessly controlling the three horses in his charge. I heard her laugh at something he said, and felt

17

a pang of discomfort. I remembered what it felt like to idolise your big brother like that.

I wondered whether maybe, for her, it would last.

2

STAR STRUCK

"You ready for this?"

I clipped up the chinstrap of my helmet and nodded, then stepped forward to take the bay mare's braided leather reins. Grace sat on the steps of the truck, watching me intently without speaking as I ran my hand down Star's glossy neck, then pulled down her stirrup and measured it against the length of my arm.

"Up or down?" Connor asked from the other side of the mare, and I looked at him over the top of the saddle.

"Up two."

He adjusted the stirrup on that side while I did mine, then checked the girth. Dad was standing off to the side with his arms folded, looking pleased as I accepted Connor's offer of a leg-up. He was having a good day. Not only had I agreed to test ride the horse he'd picked out for me, but the ponies had all jumped super in their opening rounds this morning. Skip had taken a narrow second place in the Open Table C, and Buck finished a creditable fifth, both of them jumping quick clears against some tough opposition. Then Forbes had truly outdone himself with a blistering round in the Pony 1.10m to win the class and position himself firmly at the top of the Championship leader board. We still had two more days of competing ahead of us, and anything could happen, but it was a very good start to the weekend.

I shortened the reins as Star lifted her head, her curved ears outlined in black. I gave her a pat and closed my legs against her sides, riding her forward between the trucks and out towards an empty space where I could put her through her paces.

I'd missed seeing her jump that morning, being too busy with my ponies to have time to stand around and wait for her to go. Dad had caught the tail end of it, and said she'd looked good, but she'd had three early rails and had finished mid-field. The Campbells excused the mare on account of Anna never having jumped a round on her before, and I'd decided to accept that reasoning and give her a shot. I didn't need an easy horse, anyway. I was looking for a challenge.

I trotted her on, flexing my fingers on the reins, feeling her out. Star fussed a little with her head, tossing it up and down as we moved across the short grass. My focus settled in on her, and the rest of the world faded away, leaving just me and this mare. The energy of her trot strides, the supple reins between my fingers, the arch of her neck and flex of her jaw, the rhythmic thud of her hoofbeats as we circled and halted, steadied and rode forward, learning one another's moves, each trying to understand what the other wanted.

"So what d'you think?" Dad eventually called to me as I cantered past him.

He was leaning against one of the venue's cross-country jumps, a big bold oxer, watching me intently. Grace was walking back and forth across the back rail, her arms outstretched for balance, while her father chatted to mine, no doubt filling his head with predictions of everything Star and I could achieve together. Connor was sitting casually on the other end of the jump, threatening to push Grace off every time she came near him. Their mother was back at the truck, making feeds, still in denial about the horse's potential sale.

I circled back towards them, brought Star back down to a quick trot, then eased her into a walk and let her stretch.

"She's hot all right," I told Dad, catching Connor's eye, and he winked at me. "I can't shift my weight without her reacting to it."

"Sensitive," Nigel said to my father. "All the best horses are, of course. Makes her very adjustable on course. Takes a bit of getting used to though. Like driving a Ferrari when you're used to a Honda." I saw Dad's eyes light up at the car reference, even as I wondered which of my ponies Nigel was calling a Honda. "That's what happened with Anna this morning. Just overrode her a bit early on, tried to do too much."

I could easily believe it. Star was highly reactive, but I already liked that about her. And she wasn't a pushbutton ride, which was a good thing. I'd had enough of those to last me a lifetime. Connor slid off the jump and motioned towards the warm-up area nearby, which was almost empty, with only a handful of riders left to jump in the main ring.

"Wanna try her over a fence?"

"Why not?" I held the reins lightly between my fingers as we made our way across the crushed grass. "Has she always had this bit, or is it something you put her in?"

He raised an eyebrow at me. "Don't you like it?"

"It's a bit much for her, isn't it?" I asked, looking down at the long shanks of the American gag.

"She came to us in a full cheek snaffle," Connor admitted. "But Mum hates them. Thinks they're ugly. We swapped her into a loose-ring to start with, but Grace couldn't hold her in it, so we tried a few different things and settled on this one."

"And the shadow roll?"

"Jump her over a couple of fences and you'll see why she's always had that, no matter what bit's in her mouth," he promised me as I rode into the warm-up ring.

We had to be careful not to get in the way of the competitors who were preparing to ride in the final class of the day, but pretty soon the last of them had gone in and we had the place to ourselves. I cantered Star down to a crossrail, being careful to stay still and keep out of her way. She sped up as she approached it, her ears pricked sharply forward, then launched herself into the air from half a stride out, giving the low fence masses of air.

I heard Dad hoot in appreciation, and gave Star a brief pat as I kept her cantering. Connor had raised the fence to a vertical, and I squared my shoulders and sat a little taller on the approach, holding the mare together. I still didn't want to touch her mouth with that severe bit, but I saw Connor's point about the shadow roll. As soon as Star lined up the jump, her head flew into the air. The large fluffy sheepskin over her noseband encouraged her to lower her head enough to be able to see the fence before she got there. She cleared it effortlessly, and I turned her the other way and circled back around to the oxer. It was a decent height, close to a metre twenty, and she tried to speed up again on the approach.

"Woah," I murmured, closing my hands firmly around the reins.

Star threw her head up in objection, and I vowed to put her in a different bit when we bought her. *If* we bought her. I softened my hand in sympathy and she shot forward again, rushing towards the jump. We reached it on an off-stride, and missed the opportunity to go long, finding ourselves right at the base instead on a very deep spot. I clamped my legs on to see what she'd do, to find out whether she'd refuse to jump. I wouldn't really have blamed her if she did, considering she was only about a foot in front of the fence, but she didn't. She launched herself into the air, springing off all fours like a startled cat, then stretching out over the oxer, giving it everything she had. We landed clear, and I shook my head in amazement as I regathered the reins I'd slipped mid-air, and looked at my father.

He was grinning, and I had to admit that he'd been right. This was one hell of a horse, and it looked like Dad was going to get his own way.

Again.

"Are you ready?"

I nodded, running the brush through my hair one more time before shoving it back into my bag and turning to my father.

"As I'll ever be."

He scoffed. "Don't make it sound like you're going to your execution. It's just drinks."

"Uh huh."

I picked up my puffa jacket and slid my arms into it as Dad opened the side door of our horse truck and stepped out into the cool evening air. The sun had dropped low on the horizon, bathing the show grounds in a hazy orange glow.

"You're not going to need that," Dad said as I zipped the jacket up and followed him out of the truck.

"Are you kidding? It's freezing out here."

It might have been late summer in the rest of New Zealand, but the evening temperatures in the South Island were always several degrees below what I was used to in Hawke's Bay. Dad shut the truck door behind us, and locked it before we headed over to the Campbells' truck. They'd invited us over while I was untacking Star after my ride, a casual invitation of the type that was often extended between fellow competitors at shows. Except when it came to us. We didn't socialise much, especially not these days. But Dad had accepted their offer, and I couldn't blame him. It must've been lonely for him lately, with Mum not attending shows and me spending as much time as possible in Katy's truck instead of my own. Her mother invited Dad along sometimes, but it was always a bit awkward. Besides, Deb was usually off socialising with friends of her own in the evenings, which left Dad alone in our truck, churning his way through paperwork. I'd assumed he always brought it along because he was a workaholic, but now I wondered if he wasn't just trying to keep himself busy.

"So you liked her, then?" Dad said as we made our way past the row of horse trucks parked around the ring perimeter. "Should we make them an offer?"

"Let's just hold up and see how she goes tomorrow," I told him. "No rush, right?"

He wasn't thrilled by my reluctance to commit. "Not unless they sell her to someone else before you make up your mind."

"Tell them we're interested, but we want to see how the weekend goes," I said firmly. "If it's meant to be, it'll work out."

The door to the Campbells' truck was open, and light was spilling out of it onto the grass nearby. Grace and a friend of hers tumbled out, giggling and shoving each other, until they saw Dad approaching and stopped, wide-eyed. I smiled at Grace, and she responded tentatively in kind before grabbing her friend's arm and scampering off with her in tow.

Dad strode up to the door and rapped on the side of the truck with his knuckles as he started up the stairs, as self-assured as ever as he let himself in. I followed meekly, relieved to hear him welcomed with enthusiasm by Connor's parents.

They were sitting on the leather upholstered seating, Jordan with a glass of wine in her hand and her feet up on the low table in the middle of the accommodation space, Nigel folding up the newspaper and getting to his feet to shake Dad's hand in welcome. Connor was sitting on the other end of the sofa with a bottle of beer in his hand, and he grinned at me as I came up the last step onto the faux pine flooring. He'd showered and changed into a black polo shirt that made his dark eyes look even deeper than usual and faded dark blue jeans.

He slid sideways, making a space on the end of the sofa for me, and I sat down next to him, doing my best to appear casual.

"You look nice," he said with a smile.

Okay, so much for casual. "Thanks. So do you." I cringed inwardly at myself. I've never been any good at small talk.

But Connor didn't seem to mind. "Cheers." He held out his beer bottle towards me as if to clink it against mine, then realised that I was still empty-handed. "Oh, you need a drink. What d'you want?"

"Um, what've you got?"

He tapped his mother's feet, and she moved them off the square table, which was revealed to be a drinks cooler in disguise. It was full of ice and a range of bottled beverages, most of which appeared to be of the alcoholic variety.

"Take your pick," Connor told me, and I looked vainly for something that didn't have alcohol in it. I knew what kind of reaction I'd get from Dad if I tried to drink in front of him. Eventually spying a can of Coke, I pulled that out and popped it open as Connor shut the lid.

"You *are* a good girl, aren't you?"

I glanced towards my dad and back again, and Connor grinned. "Right. I see I'm gonna have to get you away from him if we're going to have any fun."

My palm sweated against the cold can as I took a long mouthful, and then another, anything to delay having to respond to that, because I had no idea what to say. Connor just smirked at me, then leaned back against the cushions and pretended to be paying attention to what my father was saying to his parents.

It took me a moment before their conversation sank into my consciousness.

"He's been a very good pony for us. Point and shoot, nothing complicated. Never had a lame day or a bad round. Not one that was his fault, anyway," Dad added, and I frowned at him. "He'd be perfect for your little girl. Mother's dream, honestly. Couldn't be safer."

Wait, what? I shot a surprised look at Connor, who just raised his eyebrows at me and took another long swig of beer.

"We've always admired him, haven't we Nige?" Jordan was saying. "We actually looked at him for Connor before the Deverauxs bought him, but the price was a little high at the time and they outbid us." She gave a tinkling laugh, and poured herself more wine. "And we were interested when we heard he was coming back on the market, but I'm afraid you beat us to the punch that time."

Dad gave a self-satisfied smile. "We had the inside edge," he admitted. "Bruce put in a good word."

I had finally worked out what I was hearing, and interjected. "Skip's not for sale."

They all looked at me with expressions of mild surprise. Well, Dad didn't. He looked at me like I'd just said something extremely rude. I ignored his frown, and directed my comment to Jordan.

"He's not for sale until I turn seventeen. Maybe not even then."

"Be reasonable, Susie," Dad said calmly, though I could tell he was annoyed with my interruption. "We won't be keeping him once you're off ponies, and judging by what I saw today, you might be off them sooner than we'd planned." He turned back to the Campbells with a reassuring smile, as if to say *Don't worry about her, her opinion doesn't count anyway.* "Just got that Pony of the Year title to tick off the bucket list," he said smugly. "Been close a couple of times, but it keeps slipping out of our grasp."

I winced at the mention of the title class, and saw Jordan and Nigel exchange frowns. Boasting about how close we'd come to winning Pony of the Year wasn't exactly a way to gain favour with people, considering the way Pete had cruelly sabotaged my biggest opposition so that I would be more likely to win it two years ago. It hadn't worked out anyway, but it still left a bitter taste in people's mouths. I wondered how much my father had had to drink tonight. It wasn't like him to be this open with anyone, least of all people he barely knew.

"Well, we're definitely interested in Skip," Jordan said firmly, sipping more wine and redirecting the subject. "We'll touch base with you again after Pony of the Year, shall we?"

Dad nodded agreeably as I stood up, setting my half-empty Coke can on the table. "I'd better go check on the ponies."

Connor stood up too. "I'll come with you."

"That was awkward."

I huffed out an angry breath. "You think?"

"Your old man always like that?"

"Yep. Decides my life for me, and expects me to just go along with it."

"Hm." Connor led Forbes a bit closer as I leaned against Skip's shoulder while he grazed. The ponies had been fine in their yards, but I'd seized the opportunity to take them for a pick of grass instead of going back to the truck to bed, in case Dad had preceded me and was lying in wait to give me an earful. Buck had been lying down dozing, and had been very reluctant to get up when I'd suggested it, so we'd left him behind to snooze.

I'd expected Connor to go and check on his own horses, but he hadn't spared them so much as a glance as he followed me to my yards. He'd offered to walk Forbes out for me, and now we were standing in the middle of the cross-country course, letting the ponies graze on the dry grass. It was little better than eating hay, but they seemed to relish the chance to stretch their legs, and I was just happy for the chance to be alone. Well, almost alone. But the company was okay too.

"It's just so typical of him," I grumbled as Skip stopped eating for a moment, deciding to sniff my boot instead. I lifted my toe and nudged his nose, and he snorted and went back to grazing. "Just offering him to you guys without even discussing it with me. And all that crap about seeing how we go in Pony of the Year, ticking that one off the bucket list. *His* bucket list, not mine. I don't think he even realised what he was saying. *'Win the class and I'll sell your pony.'* Right, because *that's* an incentive."

27

Connor grinned at me unsympathetically. "It's gotta be time to move on though," he said. "You can't ride ponies forever, and those jumps start looking pretty small when you're doing Young Riders."

I shrugged, avoiding his eyes. "I guess they do, but I don't really care about the height. It's not about that."

"So what's it about?"

I thought for a moment. "It's about doing the best I can, on the day. Building a good enough relationship with my ponies that I can always get a solid performance out of them. With Buck and Skip, it's pretty easy. Forbes is more of a challenge, but that's what I like about him."

"Star'd be a challenge too," he reminded me.

"Yeah, that's true. And I like her. But…I don't know. I like doing the pony classes."

"Even though you don't care about winning Pony of the Year."

"Yeah. I mean, I wouldn't exactly be gutted if I won, but it's just a title at the end of the day, right? Just a rug and a sash and a bit of prize money."

"And a garland. Don't forget the garland," Connor said. "I think there's a cup, too."

I waved my hand dismissively. "But what does any of that matter, really? If it was a choice between those things and keeping my pony, I know which one I'd make."

"And here I thought you were ruthlessly competitive."

"Well, you thought wrong," I told him firmly. Maybe that had been true once, but it wasn't any more.

"I'm starting to think that there are lots of things I've been wrong about, with you." Connor came closer, Forbes's lead rope in one hand, his half-empty beer bottle held loosely in the other. "How old are you?"

I swallowed, my throat gone suddenly dry. "Fifteen."

He took another swig of beer, and wiped his mouth with the back of his hand. "You're just a baby."

"I'll be sixteen in June."

An eyebrow lifted. "Bad month for a birthday."

"I know."

He was so close to me now that I had to tilt my head back to keep looking up at him. He smiled down at me, lowered his head, and then his mouth was pressed against mine, firm and insistent. I parted my lips in surprise, and he took that as further invitation to deepen the kiss. His mouth was warm, and tasted like beer. The sensation was overwhelming, although not entirely unpleasant. I felt caught off balance, and wondered if he could tell that this was my first kiss. His mouth was everywhere, smothering mine, and I did my best to respond appropriately, blundering my way through this completely unexpected turn of events.

Forbes snorted, and Connor drew back, breaking the connection between us. He looked at me, his head tilted slightly to the side, and a slow smile crept across his face. He didn't say anything, just put his arm around my shoulders and hugged me against him for a moment. My head rested briefly against his collarbone, his breath was in my hair and his fingers tight around my upper arm. Then he let me go and stepped back, jiggling Forbes's lead rope idly in his hand.

"It's getting late. We should head back."

I nodded, my mind reeling. What was going on? Did he actually like me, or had he just done that to see if he could – to see if I'd let him? I couldn't tell, could barely see his face in the darkness as he turned away from me and started leading Forbes back towards the yards. I followed him in silence, my feet crunching on the brittle grass. Forbes's long tail swished contentedly as he walked, and I tried to wrap my head around what had just happened.

What it all meant, and where it would go from here.

3
PRACTICE FENCE

"Who d'you reckon they'll pick?"

"For what?"

"The pony team that's going to Ireland."

I turned my head slightly, my attention arrested by the other riders' conversation, and I drew Buck to a halt. Pretending to be looking over the course, I eavesdropped shamelessly on the two younger riders.

"Not me, anyway," Grace shrugged, plucking idly at one of Summer's plaits.

"They might," her friend said loyally. "More likely to pick you than me, anyway. Especially after Flame stopped twice yesterday," she added sulkily, her lower lip jutting into a pout.

I recognised her then as Grace's friend from last night. More easily, I recognised her pony Flamethrower, a flashy chestnut mare with white stockings up to her knees.

"You're still getting used to her," Grace reassured her friend. "You'll be fine."

"I wish they were taking a proper pony team, like they did two years ago," the girl complained. "Anna was telling me all about it yesterday. They had under-twelves, under-fourteens and under-sixteens. We might be in with a shot at making the team if they were doing that again, but they're only taking two under-sixteens for the pony classes. We're screwed."

The steward sent her into the ring then, and I nudged Buck up alongside Grace. She turned to look at me, and I gave her a friendly smile.

"Heya Grace."

"Oh, hi." She didn't seem thrilled to see me, but she didn't ride away either. I pretended to watch her friend in the ring for a moment. Flame jigged across the grass, tossing her head restlessly, and the kid shortened her reins, holding the feisty mare's head tightly.

"I didn't know Anna had sold Flame."

"Yeah, Issy got her for Christmas." Her voice was flat, and I couldn't tell whether she was shy, or just didn't like me. Usually I'd assume the latter, but I decided to give her the benefit of the doubt.

"She's a tough ride." I bit off the second half of that sentence. *For a kid.*

Grace glanced at me again, her dark eyebrows knitting together. "Yeah, she is." She glanced at Buck, then back at me. "Are you really retiring Buckingham after this season?"

I shrugged. "I dunno. Maybe." Buck decided to make friends with Summer, reaching over and sniffing her nose. She laid her ears back and pulled a face at him, barely suppressing a squeal. Unfazed, Buck turned his head away, deciding to mind his own business again. "So what's all this about a young rider team going to Ireland?"

Grace seemed surprised by my question. "Didn't you hear about it?"

"No." I shrugged, trying not to seem bothered. "Must be out of the loop."

Grace looked a bit cagey, but nodded. "It's for a team competition in June. You have to be under-sixteen to make the team," she added, looking at me through narrowing eyes. "At least, for the Juniors you do. They're taking two under-eighteen riders as well, and two under-twenty-ones. At least, that's what Mum said."

"Connor planning to go?"

She shrugged. "Mum wants him to, but he'll have hockey then and he doesn't want to miss any tournaments."

"I didn't know he played hockey."

"Yeah, he's on the National Junior Development squad. He does heaps of training for it. That's why he's only got two horses this season. Doesn't have time to work any more than that."

"Right." Everyone had a life outside of horses, it would seem. Everyone except me. I cast my mind back over what Grace had said. "When in June is it?"

"Right at the start, I think. Just before the school holidays start."

I grinned, relieved. I wouldn't be sixteen until the end of June. I was about to ask more when Grace's mum turned up at the gate to check that her daughter knew the course. She said a brief hello to me, and I wished Grace luck as I rode Buck away to finish his warm-up.

I knew that Dad would be all over this team thing as soon as he found out about it. His biggest ambitions for me all revolved around getting into a New Zealand team. He wanted so desperately to see that silver fern patch stitched onto the front of my competition jacket, and he'd been gutted when I'd never qualified for the Children's FEI Final in the past, despite coming close a couple of times.

I squeezed Buck up into a trot, flexing my fingers on the reins as I asked him to go forward and bend around my leg. I'd never been to Ireland. I wondered what it was like, and who else was going to be gunning for a place on the team.

Katy, for starters. She sent me a text that afternoon to find out if I'd heard about it, and whether I was planning on putting my name forward. I texted her back straight away.

Yep. Just sneak in age-wise bc it ends a week before my birthday! Dads all over it like a rash haha. I hope we both get to go!!

I hit Send and shoved my phone back in my pocket, then finished buckling Forbes's open-fronted tendon boots. Straightening up, I gave him a clap on the shoulder and looked him in the eye.

"Right, boy. You ready for this?"

Dad had his head bent over his paperwork as I stepped up into the truck to get my jacket. Despite last night's chill, it was blisteringly hot today, and Forbes was sweating just standing around. I'd waited as long as I could before tacking him up for the class, but he needed a long warm-up, and I wasn't going to change our routine now. I'd just work him a little slower than usual, that was all. I grabbed my favourite burgundy jacket and slung it over my arm. Time enough to put that on when I was about to go into the ring.

"Coming?"

Dad wrote something else on a piece of paper, then set down his pen. "You ready to go?"

I nodded. "Yep." My phone buzzed in my pocket, and I pulled it out and read Katy's text as I went back outside.

Yeah thatd be sweet! Saw results on FB this morning, good work Skipper! What happened to Buck tho?

I smiled at the first part, then cringed at her second question. Skip had jumped a super double clear earlier to pick up another second placing and secure us the top spot on the overall leader board, but Buck had had a refusal at the wall, putting himself out of contention.

Had a stop. Not sure why. Its stinking hot down here tho and the grounds hard as rock so prob just feeling it on the old joints. Have scratched him from the rest of the show and will get him looked at when we get home

Dad made an impatient noise in the back of his throat as I sent the text, then shoved my phone into my pocket and kicked my left leg up for a leg-up. I waited for him to say something, or make me hand my phone over to him, but he didn't. He grabbed my calf with one hand and boosted me into the saddle, then gave Forbes a pat on the neck before turning away to lock the truck behind us.

I tightened my girth as Forbes walked over to the ring, Dad

strolling along at my side. All around us people greeted each other, waving and chatting and catching up with one another's results. But nobody stopped me, or said hello, or asked me how my day was going. Forbes strode through them all like Moses parting the Red Sea, and I missed Katy and AJ, the only people who made me feel like a person and not like a leper.

I rode past the Campbells' truck, where Grace was sitting on the ramp with her friend Issy. Seemingly unperturbed by the disastrous rounds they'd both had this morning, they were giggling over something on Grace's iPad. Nearby, Jordan crouched next to her daughter's pony, rubbing liniment onto Summertime's legs. Issy's mother was probably fussing over Flame in an equal manner, both parents working overtime to ensure that their children had a chance to compete at top level, although neither of them seemed ready for it yet. I gave myself a mental kick, knowing that only a couple of years ago, I'd been no different. Worse, probably, because I'd thought I knew it all. Thought it only took better ponies and more determination, missing out on the empathy side of the equation altogether. The last two years had taught me otherwise, and despite how hard it had been to fall so far, I wouldn't trade what I knew now for anything.

"So have you given the bay mare any more thought?" Dad broke into my thoughts, and I looked down at him. He tilted his head towards me, the sun reflecting off his polished sunglasses.

I kept my tone ambivalent. "I watched her go this morning," I said. "Jumped pretty well."

Actually, *pretty well* was an understatement. Star had cleared everything with room to spare, and there'd been several people on the sidelines admiring her. She'd been quick around the jump off too, just taking one rail at the second to last fence. I'd seen it coming as Anna had turned the corner, letting Star get a bit quick and not sitting her back on her hocks enough. She'd underestimated the length of the little mare's stride, and by the time she'd realised her error, they'd been too close to the fence. Star had given it everything, but she'd rubbed the back rail of the oxer as she angled over it. She'd given Anna a good couple of bucks on landing, telling her off, and Anna had corrected her ride to finish the course, but it left them out of the ribbons in the highly-competitive class. With yesterday's mixed result added to today's, they wouldn't be qualified for the Final tomorrow.

Dad echoed that conclusion as we reached the warm-up. "Nigel was saying earlier that they've late-entered her into the non-championship class tomorrow afternoon, since she didn't qualify. Offered to let you take her round." He couldn't keep the enthusiasm out of his voice any longer, but I wasn't so keen.

"Maybe."

"What d'you mean, maybe?" Dad was frowning at me now. He stopped in the gate of the warm-up ring, putting a hand on Forbes's rein to hold him still. "I thought you liked her."

"I do. I just…" I ground my teeth together, then confessed. "I don't want to screw it up."

"You won't." There was such certainty in his voice. I wished I shared his confidence in me. "Rode her beautifully yesterday, didn't you?"

"She went okay. But it's different in the ring. Everyone will be watching, and…"

Dad clenched his jaw, betraying his impatience with me. "Susie, you've got to get over that," he told me firmly. "Besides, it'll be good practice for you to compete on a horse you've hardly ridden. That's what you'll have to do in Ireland, so you might as well get some practice in now."

"I haven't made the team yet," I reminded him, but he scoffed.

"Bruce is a selector. He knows you, knows how well you ride," Dad said, his voice assured. "I'll have a chat with him, make sure he knows how badly we want it."

I heard the certainty in his voice, and knew that if money had to change hands to get me on that team, that he'd make that happen too. The thought of it made me shiver. I didn't want to make the team if that's what it would take. I wanted to be selected on merit, not on bank balance, and I was about to tell him that when we were interrupted.

"You're blocking the gate."

I looked up to see Anna in front of us, waiting to get out of the warm-up and into the ring. "Oh, sorry."

I nudged Forbes out of the way and she rode by with a frosty demeanour. I wondered if she'd overheard Dad's last comment, and whether she'd interpreted it the same way I had. Anna was almost certainly going to put her name forward for the team, and had a high chance of being selected. Her parents were wealthy and she was ambitious, and with a couple of international team competitions already under her belt, she was almost a sure thing. At least she was over sixteen, so we weren't competing for the same spot.

I sent Forbes straight into a trot and rode away from my father. He was right, as much as I always hated to admit it. I did have to practice riding unknown horses and ponies before a team event like that. And that was one thing Katy definitely had on her side. She'd grown up riding different ponies, picking up catch rides all the time, and everyone knew that she could get almost anything to go well. Forbes was the only tricky pony I'd ever had – all the others had come to me fully-trained. And even he had come to me with most of his quirks already ironed out.

Our class was running in reverse order of points, which meant that after yesterday's win, Forbes and I would be last to go. It was the final class of the day, and the warm-up steadily emptied out as I worked my pony in. Forbes always took a good half-hour to get really switched on. I had to be careful today though, as despite the later hour, it wasn't getting any cooler. The sun baked down onto the scorched earth, and Forbes was sweating heavily as I brought him back to a walk and gave him a pat.

Dad was over at the practice fence, putting the vertical down to a crossrail and motioning to me to come and jump it. In a burst of defiance, I reached into my pocket and pulled out my phone, wanting to check first whether Katy had replied to my text.

Aw poor old Bucky. Give him a hug for me, and tell Skip to kick ass tomorrow!!!

I slipped it back into my jacket and picked up my reins as I rode past the practice jump, ignoring Dad's glare. There were three other riders still in the warm-up, and I scanned them quickly, trying to figure out the order of go. I knew the boy on the chestnut-and-white pinto would be going in right before me, and since the roan had just been called into the ring, I figured the liver chestnut would be up next. We were only two away now, and I pushed Forbes up into a trot as a young girl with blonde hair pulled back into a tight ponytail came over to the crossrail and started adjusting it back into a vertical. Dad quit glaring at me and directed his annoyance towards her instead.

"Hey, leave that alone! We're using it."

The girl looked at my father with a frown, and I recognised her in a vague sort of way. She had just started show jumping this season, but after a couple of shaky rounds early on, she'd made massive strides lately and was climbing quickly up the Pony Grand Prix leader board after a succession of recent wins. Of course, she had a pair of very experienced ponies that could probably jump clear rounds with their eyes closed, which definitely helped. But then, who was I to judge?

"Emmalee wants to jump it," the girl, whose name I still couldn't remember, told my father. She seemed slightly cowed by Dad's aggressive tone, but she was standing her ground. "She's next to go in, and she wants to do a vertical first."

Dad folded his arms across his chest, glowering down at her. "My daughter hasn't even jumped yet," he countered. "Your friend's had ample time to jump the vertical, now it's Susannah's turn."

I saw the girl's eyes flicker towards me, then back to my father. "But…"

"But nothing. It's not your turn," he insisted.

She opened her mouth to speak, then clearly thought better of it, turning around and walking back towards a group of people standing by the gate. I wanted to say something, to apologise for my father and counteract his bullying, but I also knew a lost cause when I saw one. I didn't have the time or the energy to fight that girl's battles for her – I had a pony to warm up. I nudged Forbes into a canter, trying to project outward calm. I knew my pony well enough to know that if I got wound up, he'd sense it and start getting wild and unmanageable, and I didn't need that today.

I cantered him over the crossrail once, landed left, and cantered back around to jump it again. But now Dad was standing in front of the jump, his arms still folded, while another man yelled at him, his arms waving angrily.

I brought Forbes back to a trot and circled him, trying to concentrate on steadying my breathing, and not letting any of the tension in the air transmit itself to Forbes. But it was too late. He tossed his head, tugging at the bit, then spooked sideways as the pinto pony came cantering past us.

"It's okay, buddy." I reached forward and gave Forbes a pat, then glanced back over at my Dad, who was still engaged in a stand-off with the other man. I couldn't hear what they were saying, but it was evident from their body language that neither one of them wanted to back down.

I wanted to ride over there and tell my father to just put the jump back to how it had been and give Emmalee a chance to jump it. The rider about to go into the ring had priority over the practice fence, and I wished Dad would just back down and accept that. The

38

blonde girl was standing over by the gate, looking a bit emotional, and I remembered her name at last. Lily Christianson. One of the women there had her arm around her shoulders, and they glared at me as they saw me looking at them. I looked away, pushing Forbes back into a canter and focusing on my pony. There was nothing else I could do. If I went over there and told Dad to give in, he'd never let me hear the end of it. He was already grumpy with me, and I didn't need to give him any more fuel for his fire. He hated it when I disagreed with him in public, even when he was clearly wrong. I just had to get Forbes into the ring and jump a clear round, followed by a quick jump off, and Dad would forget to be angry with me.

But that was looking less and less likely to happen, because I couldn't stop myself from tensing up, and Forbes couldn't handle it. He got quicker and quicker as we cantered around the warm-up, and when I tried to slow him down, he flung his head from side to side and lifted his back, threatening to buck.

The call came from the steward, sounding terse. "Emmalee, the judges are waiting for you. You need to get over to the ring right away. Isaac, you're on straight after her, and Susannah's last to go." She looked up from her clipboard and finally noticed the stand-off happening in front of the practice fence. A frown crossed her sun-creased face. "What's going on here?"

I drew Forbes back to a walk, bracing myself for further drama as the small group at the gate quickly filled her in on the situation. The steward looked furious as she slapped her clipboard against her thigh.

"Well we're out of time. Emmalee needs to get into the ring right now or they'll disqualify her for not turning up."

Emmalee's mother started arguing that her daughter needed to jump the vertical before she could go into the ring, but the steward wasn't having a bar of it. Defeated, Emmalee rode her pretty liver chestnut out towards the ring, and her mother followed with a scowl as I halted Forbes and checked my girth. Any excuse to keep my eyes down and avoid looking at anyone. Dad was still going at it with Lily's father, their conversation carrying across the dusty warm-up as both men talked over top of each other, much to the steward's obvious irritation.

"Would you two give it a rest?" she snapped finally, and for a wonder they stopped yelling. "It's done. Derrick, the practice fence is yours. Hugh, can we talk?"

She led the other man away, nodding sympathetically to his furious tirade, as Dad turned towards me with a pleased expression, thinking he'd won.

"Okay Susie. It's all yours."

I could still feel their eyes on me as I rode into the ring. I'd had to walk Forbes past Emmalee, who was sitting on her pony by the gate and dabbing at tears while her mother patted her leg and told her that it wasn't her fault. My heart sank. I'd been hoping that she'd have pulled off a clear round despite the practice fence drama, and that it would all become a moot point. But clearly she hadn't, and I could tell from the look on her mother's face that she was already on the war path against me.

"That's all clear in the jump-off and a very smart time for Isaac Winton and Puzzle Time, putting them into second place, just behind our current leader," the announcer said as I rode Forbes into the ring. "We now welcome the last rider to go in the second round of the Pony Metre-Ten Championship, Susannah Andrews riding Primo Del Maestro."

Isaac trotted his pony past me to the gate, and I sent Forbes into a canter, waiting for the buzzer. I'd caught the end of Isaac's jump off while I waited, and he hadn't been wasting any time out here, so whoever was leading the class must have really carved it up. I wondered idly who it had been, and whether Forbes could go fast enough to beat their time. But I couldn't get ahead of myself. We had to jump a clear first round, and only then could I think about the instant jump-off. The announcer was thinking along the same lines, telling the crowd that I needed to jump a fast double clear to keep my position at the top of the rankings.

No pressure, I thought ruefully. But then, maybe it was good. If I made it onto the team going to Ireland, I was going to have to be able to ride under pressure. *Imagine you're in a team right now*, I told myself. *Imagine that you need this to go well for their sakes.*

The thought spurred me on, and as the buzzer sounded, I drew my shoulders back, sank my weight down into my heels and steadied my pony on our way to the first fence. Forbes was still a bit unsettled, and he sped up on the approach and flung himself into the air, clearing the first jump by miles. I sat up quickly, bringing my body upright even before his front feet had touched the ground again, ready to balance and steady him. He tugged at the reins on landing, but I had enough core strength to hold him, and got the steady six strides we needed down to the second fence. He jumped that one huge too, but at least he wasn't touching them.

On, and on we went around the course. Five fences to go, then four, then three. Forbes cleared the Swedish oxer with a kick of his heels, and I looked around to the left towards the big, airy white vertical coming up next. From the corner of my eye, I glimpsed Emmalee and her family still standing at the gate watching us, and felt a jolt of guilt.

It only lasted for a second, but it was enough to distract Forbes, and he hit the brakes so hard that if I hadn't already been working hard to balance him around the corner, I'd have gone straight over his head. As it was, I was thrown forward onto his neck, bruising my chest as my upper body connected with his hard crest.

I regained my seat and wrapped my legs firmly around his sides, trying to put the spook behind us and focusing hard on the fence that lay only a few strides ahead. But Forbes stood still, his hooves planted to the ground, and refused to move. My heart sank as I realised what was happening. I'd seen him do this before with Katy – dig his toes in and refuse, point blank, to go forward. I dug my spurs into his sides and growled at Forbes, telling him to get a move on. I didn't carry a crop, so I couldn't have given him a smack even if I'd wanted to, which I didn't. Katy had tried that once, and he'd started rearing. I didn't want that to happen, but I was running out of options.

I nudged him harder, and risked a small kick, despite the spurs. But nothing worked, and as I started to really panic, a voice yelled from behind me.

"Spin him in a circle!"

I had no idea who it was, and no time to figure it out. I just grabbed my left rein and brought it around towards my knee, taking their advice. Before he could work out what was happening, Forbes's nose was touching my boot. He tugged at the rein, but I was one step ahead of him at last, and I tucked my hand behind my knee to prevent him from pulling the rein out of my hand. He spun his hindquarters around, trying to align his body with his neck, but it wasn't until we were lined up towards the white vertical that I released his head. Before he had time to think about what had just happened, I clamped my legs onto his sides and rode him firmly forward. He leapt into a canter, then baulked at the sight of the jump ahead.

"Geddup!" I growled at him, giving him another kick with my heels, and he shot forward, flinging himself over the high vertical. I felt him flatten out through the air, and heard his hooves clatter against the top rail, then the thud as it fell. *Damn.*

No time to worry about that though, because we had the triple bar still to jump. I sat up and turned him towards it, and he backed off sulkily. I knew he didn't like the way I was riding him, bullying him into jumping when he'd decided that he'd had enough, but it wasn't up to him to decide that. I pushed him forward as strongly as I could, and despite his reluctance, Forbes cantered up to the last fence, almost refused, then begrudgingly jumped it, stalling in midair before coming down on top of the back rail. It fell to the ground as my pony cantered stiffly through the finish flags, his ears laid flat back against his glossy neck.

I brought Forbes straight back to a walk, feeling the hitch in his stride. *Damn, damn, damn.* He must've really bashed it his leg on that last jump. I patted him effusively, since he'd done as he was told in the end, letting the reins go slack as I rubbed both sides of his neck the way he liked. Dad met me at the gate, shaking his head.

"He hit that last one pretty hard," I commented, trying not to mention the napping incident, which would fire Dad up much more than a rail or two. Rails were disappointing, but bad behaviour was unforgivable.

"Got it with his stifle," Dad said flatly. "Guess he's still got some growing up to do. Walk him out."

He gave Forbes a cursory slap on the neck as I dismounted and loosened the girth. Forbes rested his off hind leg as I ran up his stirrups, and I watched anxiously as I led him forward, hoping he'd be okay for tomorrow. Despite that disaster, he could still be in the top few to go into the final round, but I wouldn't be jumping him if he wasn't one hundred percent sound. It wasn't worth the risk.

4
NOT THAT GIRL

"How's your pony?"

I turned at the sound of Connor's voice, and smiled tentatively as he approached me through the dusky twilight. He had a cap pulled down over his dark hair, and his black singlet showed off his broad, muscular shoulders. Not to mention his biceps, and I quickly forced myself to look at his face. He was grinning at me, appearing amused, and I felt my skin flush.

"Um, a bit sore. But I think he'll be okay." I ran my hand again over Forbes's stifle, the liniment on my hand making my skin tingle. He lifted his leg and swished his tail threateningly at me, and I desisted.

"That's good. Little bastard, napping on you like that."

"Yeah, well." I shrugged. "One of his less endearing quirks. He used to do it to Katy all the time, but it's the first time he's pulled it on me."

"I remember. Thought you were nuts for buying him, to be honest. But you got him going and made him finish the course, so maybe he won't try it again."

"Here's hoping." I threw a cover over Forbes and clipped up the backstraps. Connor let himself into my pony's yard and started buckling the front for me.

"I always told Katy to spin him too, but she never did," Connor said as he pulled Forbes's neck rug up to his ears. "Stubborn, that girl. Won't listen to good advice." He was still grinning at me as it clicked.

"That was you?"

"Who'd you think it was?"

I shrugged. "I had no idea, only that it worked."

"Well, yeah. That was yours truly. And you're welcome."

"Thanks," I said belatedly. "It was definitely…"

But I was interrupted by a loud cough from behind me, making me jump. Turning, I saw Buck standing in his yard with his head low, and as I watched, he coughed again, his whole body racked with the convulsion.

"You okay, buddy?" I asked the pony, ducking through the railings to get into his yard. Buck lifted his head and pricked his ears at me, then coughed again. It wasn't a dry cough, like he sometimes got when he'd had too much dry hay, or had something stuck in his throat. It was a wet, thick cough, and my blood chilled at the sound.

Connor was right behind me, frowning as he echoed my thoughts. "That doesn't sound too good."

"No, it doesn't." Buck shook his head, then blew out through his nostrils, covering both of us with a spray of horse snot.

"Nice. Cheers mate," Connor muttered, but I was too busy running my hand down Buck's neck and chest, checking to see if he was sweating. He seemed fine, and far less concerned than I was. Buck cleared his nose again, then nuzzled me gently.

"He seems okay now," Connor said. "Must've just had something in his throat."

"Hmm. Maybe." I wasn't convinced, but I wanted Connor to be right. I checked Buck's nose for any discharge, but there was nothing obvious. Then again, he'd just sprayed it all over me and Connor. Twice.

"He'll be right." Connor took his cap off and ruffled his dark hair, successfully distracting me from my pony's plight. "Hey, what're you up to tonight?"

I shrugged. "Not much." *Absolutely nothing,* was the actual truth,

45

but I didn't want to say that out loud for fear of sounding like a total loser.

"Come over to our truck, if you want," he suggested. "I've got some videos of Star jumping in Aussie that you might wanna see."

"Okay, sure," I said, trying to sound casual. "When?"

He shrugged. "Whenever. I'm going to check on our lot, then I'll head back over. Half an hour, maybe?"

I nodded, rubbing Buck's warm ears. "Sounds good. See you soon."

I took a deep breath, then pulled out my Ariat jacket and slipped it on. Dad looked up from his phone conversation with a frown.

"Hang on a sec," he said to the person he was talking to, then looked at me. "Where are you off to?"

"The Campbells' truck," I told him. "They've got some videos of Star competing in Aussie that they were going to show me."

Dad's expression eased. "Oh, right. I said to Jordan that you'd want to see those. She showed me last night."

I nodded. "Great. I'll see you later then." I opened the side door of our truck and started down the steps.

"Susie."

I turned to face him. "What?"

"Don't be back too late. You've got a class first thing in the morning."

"I know. I won't be."

He nodded, then turned his attention back to his phone conversation. "Right, where were we?"

I jumped onto the grass and shut the door behind me. There were lights on in all the trucks that I passed, and voices issuing from them. Music, and laughter. And now I was going to join them. It was still a novelty to me to be able to leave our truck in the evenings at all, let alone to go and hang out with other people. Especially without Dad tagging along. For years, I'd barely been allowed out of my parents' sight when we were away competing. Pete had been given more of a free pass, on account of being both several years older than me and a boy, but I'd been cosseted and kept close. And the first time my parents *had* let me leave the truck, I'd been stupid enough to pick a fight and ended up with a mild concussion, so that was the last time I'd been given free rein to roam the show grounds at night.

Until now.

I turned the corner towards where the Campbells were parked, then stopped, feeling incredibly stupid. The truck was dark, the ramp was up and the doors firmly closed. Nobody was in there, and I was glad that the receding daylight hid the blush on my skin as I realised that I'd been taken in. It was stupid of me, really, to think that Connor actually wanted to spend time with me. He was probably sitting in Anna's truck right now, laughing about my naivety in thinking that I'd actually made a friend.

Stupid, stupid, stupid.

I turned on my heel and decided to go and check on my ponies again. I couldn't go straight back to our truck, not with Dad sitting there. He'd want to know why I was back so soon, and I'd have to come up with some excuse, because if I told him the truth, he'd go charging off to defend me. And of all the things in the world that I didn't need right now, I definitely didn't need that.

"Susannah!"

I spun around to see Connor striding towards me, looking puzzled. "Where're you going?"

"Um…" I motioned towards his dark truck. "I didn't know where you were, so…" I let the sentence trail off, and he grimaced.

"Took longer to sort my horses out than I expected. Grace didn't fill up the water buckets like I told her to, and Rex had the wrong rug on and was sweating like a demon under it, and then Summer choked on her hay…" He threw his hands up in despair. "Always

47

something, eh?"

I smiled, retracing my steps in his direction. "Yeah, tell me about it. Is Summer okay?"

"Oh yeah, she's fine. I took the hay off her and left it to soak, so I've just gotta remember to give it back to her later on." He was walking back towards his truck as he spoke, and reached up to open the side door. "C'mon in."

He flicked the lights on as we entered the truck, and I shut the door behind me as I followed.

"Where is everyone?"

"At the Jessops' tonight," he said, opening the coffee-table-drinks-cooler in the middle of the room and pulling out two glass bottles. "Their turn to feed the hordes. Cheers."

Connor popped the lid off one of the bottles, and held it out to me. I didn't want to be rude, so I took it. I could smell the alcohol mixed with the sickly sweet lemon fizz, but wasn't sure how to tell him that I didn't drink without sounding like a complete loser. Connor clinked his own bottle against mine, then raised it to his lips, watching me as he took a long swallow. I gave in and followed suit, letting the cold liquid slide down my throat. I was thirstier than I'd realised, and the strong taste of lemon almost cancelled out the unfamiliar taste of the alcohol.

Almost.

"Sit down, and I'll find that video for you."

I did as I was told, taking a seat amongst the jackets and potato chip packets and piles of show catalogues that were scattered around on the leather sofa. Connor was rummaging around in the corner, muttering under his breath as he looked for something. It was warm in the truck, and I unzipped my jacket and took it off, revealing the lacy white top that I'd put on underneath.

"Where'd she put it? Oh, here."

He pulled out an iPad in a bright pink case, and I raised my eyebrows at him as I took another long, cold drink. I was getting used to the taste. And I could get used to the way Connor was looking at me, his eyes roving appreciatively over the cleavage that the top showed. I'd debated whether to wear it or pick something a little more casual, but I was glad now that I'd made what was clearly the right choice.

Connor cleared his throat and looked down at the iPad in his hands.

"Not mine, obviously," he assured me, sitting down right next to me and putting his feet up on the coffee table. I watched his long fingers swipe across the iPad screen, searching for the right files. His shoulder was warm against mine, and he was sitting so close that our hips were touching.

"Here." He crossed his legs, pressing his thigh against mine, and turned slightly in my direction. "This is her at the Young Horse Champs in Aussie last year."

He took another long drink as the video started to play. It was a bit fuzzy and the screen was smudged with fingerprints, so it took me a moment to pick out Star in amongst the jumps. I sipped at the drink in my hand as the camera zoomed in and found her, and she made her way around the course. The little mare jumped well, springing cleanly over every fence and finishing the course with a clear round.

"What d'you think?"

"Nice," I said. "She looks good."

"Your type of horse, I reckon." He swiped off the screen, then scrolled through the files, looking for something else. "There's another one here somewhere. Aha."

I leaned back against the cushions and watched Star schooling at what had clearly been her previous home. The sand arena was surrounded by gum trees, and the sound of her hooves crunching against the surface was occasionally interrupted by the screech of raucous birds. This video was better quality, and I leaned my head back against the wall as I watched. That changed the angle, though, and I reached over and tilted the screen in my direction.

Connor moved his hand so that our fingers brushed against each other. He turned his head and I could hear the smile in his voice, could feel his breath against my skin as he spoke.

"Better?"

I nodded, then took another swallow of the drink, realising that somehow, I'd drunk the whole thing already.

"Ready for a refill?" Connor asked, taking the empty bottle from my hand and pressing the iPad into my lap as he moved his feet and flipped up the coffee table lid.

"Uh…" I wasn't sure how much alcohol was in those drinks, but any at all would be more than I was used to, and I didn't think I should drink too much more. "Maybe just a Coke."

Connor looked guilty as he held out another bottle towards me. "Sorry, I already opened it. And I think we're out of Coke. Gracie drinks the stuff like it's going off the market. But I can get you some water, if you want?"

I shook my head, not wanting to be a nuisance, and took the drink from him. One more couldn't hurt, and I didn't even feel any different after the first one. The alcohol content was probably pretty low. "It's fine. Thanks."

Connor grinned at me again as he sat back against the sofa cushions, and this time he put his arm across the back of the sofa, his fingertips brushing my shoulder. I swallowed down another long gulp of the sweet drink, and repositioned the iPad on my lap. This time it was Connor's turn to adjust it slightly, so that he could see it too.

"That okay?" he asked. I could tell he was looking at me, so I turned my head and smiled at him.

"Yeah, fine."

Star trotted across the screen, but neither of us were watching her any more. Connor's eyes were locked on mine, and he raised one hand to brush the back of his fingers against my cheek. I wondered, weirdly, what he'd done with the drink he'd just had in his hand, then forgot about that as he leaned in and kissed me.

I'd spent all of last night wondering what he'd meant by that first kiss. Whether he'd planned it, or if it had been spur of the moment. Whether he actually liked me, or had just been doing it to see if he could. Whether he'd want more, or whether one kiss would be enough.

That question, at least, had just been answered. I kissed him back carefully, nervously, hoping I was doing it right. Hoping he couldn't tell how inexperienced I was. Trying to think less, and just live in the moment, letting my instincts take over.

He was smiling when we eventually broke apart, cupping the side of my face in the palm of his hand. His thumb traced a lazy line across my cheekbone, and I felt my brain get even fuzzier than it was already feeling. Maybe there was something in that bottle that was affecting me after all.

"You're so pretty." I blinked at him, and he looked surprised. "What, you don't think you're pretty?"

"I..." How was I supposed to answer that question? I knew I wasn't ugly, but to agree with him would sound like vanity. I clamped my mouth shut, then noticed his laughing expression.

"Shut up."

He chuckled. "Well in case you're wondering, you are." He leaned in and kissed me again, softly, on the lips. "Very, very pretty," he murmured.

Then his mouth moved down my neck, and I could feel my whole body start to tingle. Connor's lips were on my collarbone now, and I was struggling to stay sitting up under the pressure of his weight leaning against me. I braced myself slightly, and he murmured again.

"Lie back."

I turned my head, glancing behind me at the pile of his family's belongings covering the sofa cushions. "Uh…"

Connor raised his head and saw my predicament. Propping himself up on one knee, he leaned right over me and used his free arm to sweep all of it onto the floor.

"That's better. Now…"

And he was pushing me back until I was lying on the sofa, and he was half up against it, half on top of me. His lanky body was pressed against the back of the sofa, and his long legs lay over mine. And then he was kissing me again, and I stopped thinking about anything other than the weight of him, the sensation of his skin so close to mine, the heady smell of his deodorant, the slight tang of sweat underneath it. His hair brushed my neck as his lips traced the line of my collarbone, and his hand slid over my stomach, his calluses snagging on the soft fabric. Then his hand was touching my breast, and I tensed up involuntarily, until his mouth was over mine again, kissing me intensely, and I let go of my inhibitions. I'd never been that kind of girl before, but maybe I could be tonight.

Maybe it was time to live a little.

I moved my own hands, sliding them up the back of his shirt and feeling the heat of his smooth, bare skin as I pulled him in closer towards me. He responded by kissing me harder, then shifted more of his weight over top of me.

Just go with it. Be that girl.

My breath was coming faster now, and Connor's hand was underneath my top and sliding across bare skin. My body was responding to him in all the right ways, but my brain couldn't keep up with it.

I can't.

I squirmed and turned my head aside, breaking our kiss. Connor pulled back, looking down at me with a furrowed brow.

"You okay?"

I nodded. "Yeah, I just…"

"We'll go slow," he said. "Sorry. I got a bit carried away, but you just…" His hands were still all over me, his hips pressed against mine. I swallowed hard as he leaned in and softly kissed my cheek. "You're just so damn pretty, it's hard to stop kissing you."

As if to prove his point, he kissed me again as he slid his hand back down to my hip and pulled me up against him. I sucked in a breath, and he smiled.

"You like that?" he asked, shifting his weight again, bringing us closer together still.

"I…" I pulled back from him, trying to get my head straight.

It was all moving too fast now, and I had no experience with any of it. But he just kept kissing me, not giving me a chance to think too much about what was going on. My head was fuzzy, and he was warm, and everything was slightly hazy around the edges. I didn't think I was drunk, not properly, but it wasn't easy to get my head straight. Not with him kissing me like that, and then suddenly I realised that he'd unbuttoned my jeans, and his hand was moving lower, and I jerked away from him.

"Stop!"

Connor broke our kiss, but he didn't move his hand. "It's okay. You're okay. Just relax."

He leaned in to kiss me again, trying to distract me, but my internal panic button was on full alert. I squirmed away from him, trying to sit up, but he was a lot taller and heavier than I was, and his weight kept me pinned to the leather seat.

"Let me go!"

He moved his hand at last, but he didn't let me up. His body weight continued to hold me down as he frowned at me, his disappointment turning to annoyance.

"Don't freak out, jeez. We're having a good time, that's all. Just chill."

But the moment of my own indecision was well and truly gone. I needed to get up and get away from him. I put a hand on his shoulder and pushed him, trying to get him off me, but he wouldn't budge. If anything, he leaned more heavily on me, as if proving that he was stronger than I was, and that I was at his mercy. For a horrifying moment I felt utterly powerless, and fear washed over me as I wondered whether I should try screaming. Would anyone even hear me?

It was worth a shot. "Get off!" I shouted the words as loudly as I could, pummelling ineffectively at his broad shoulder, desperate to be free.

Connor gave me a disgusted look, but he shifted his weight at last, and I moved quickly, sliding out from underneath him and onto my knees on the vinyl-coated floor. I scrambled to my feet and swiftly buttoned my jeans, feeling my hands shaking as I did.

"We were just having a bit of fun." Connor leaned back against the cushions, one arm still across the back of the sofa, looking completely nonchalant.

"That wasn't fun."

He rolled his eyes. "Oh, come on. Don't act like you didn't want it."

"I...what?"

"You came here alone, dressed like that." He waved a hand in my direction, and I felt my skin crawl at the thought of him touching me again. "You must've known what was going to happen."

I stared at him, horrified. "What? *No.* I came here to see videos of Star."

But even as I spoke, I wondered if he was right. I'd worn the lacy top because it was pretty, and because it showed off some cleavage. I'd planned for him to see it. And I'd kissed him back, and let him undress me, at least partway. That meant I'd wanted more. Didn't it? But he'd crossed the line of what I was comfortable with, and he hadn't stopped when I'd told him to. Well, he'd stopped, but not right away. My head swirled, and I felt dizzy and sick to my stomach. I had to get out of that truck. I took a step towards the door as Connor picked up his half-empty bottle from the floor and took a gulp, then wiped his mouth with the back of his hand.

"Fine, piss off then. If I'd known you were such a little tease, I wouldn't have bothered with you in the first place."

He picked my jacket up off the floor and threw it at me. The zipper hit me in the lip, and it stung. I blinked furiously as tears prickled the corners of my eyes. *Do. Not. Cry. Not in front of him.* I fumbled at the door handle, my hands shaking. *Get out. Get out get out get out.* I finally got the catch to open, and stumbled down the steps into the cool night air.

I left the door open behind me. Let Connor get up and shut it himself. I walked fast, wanting to put as much distance between myself and him as possible. My legs were shaking, and the world around me seemed to be tilting. How much had I had to drink?

I stopped at last outside our large silver truck. The lights were still on, which meant Dad was still awake. I wondered if he'd be able to smell the alcohol on me. I wondered what else he'd be able to tell.

I turned around and went towards the yards instead, going the long way around so that I wouldn't have to walk back past Connor's truck. My ponies were dozing in their yards. Skip and Forbes were standing up, but Buck was lying down, flat on his side and breathing heavily.

"Hi boys."

Skip opened his eyes sleepily and whiffled his nostrils at me. Forbes twitched an ear back and forth, and otherwise ignored me. Buck slept on. I gave Skip a quick rub between his eyes, then left him to sleep, slipping instead into Buck's yard.

"How you doing, old man?" He didn't notice as I sat down near his head, resisting the temptation to wake him. He was sleeping soundly, and I rested my chin on my knees and closed my eyes, listening to the soothing sound of his deep, slow breaths.

How could I have been so stupid as to think that Connor actually liked me? That he actually had some interest in me, and wasn't just chasing another conquest? I'd known what he was like, had known better than to get involved with his games. And yet I'd fallen for them all, hook, line and sinker. I'd made an idiot of myself, and I hugged my knees tighter, dreading what tomorrow was going to bring.

5

NATIONAL DISASTER

I made it back to the truck eventually and brushed my teeth before Dad had a chance to smell any alcohol on my breath, scrubbed the makeup off my face before he could notice the smeared mascara on my cheeks, and changed into my pyjamas with hardly a word to him. He was distracted by his work, and kept running his hand through his greying hair, putting his reading glasses on and then taking them off again, and muttering to himself.

I was thinking longingly of my bed – right up until I crawled into it. *Safe at last*, I told myself, snuggling down and closing my eyes tightly, cocooning myself amongst the familiar warmth and weight of heavy blankets. But I couldn't relax, let alone fall asleep. I shifted around constantly, tossing and turning until Dad asked whether there were fleas in my bed. I assured him that there weren't, and did my best to lie still.

Lie back.

I shivered, and pressed my face into my pillow. My lip stung, and I knew it was swollen where the zipper had hit it.

You're overreacting, I told myself. *What actually happened?*

Nothing.

Too much.

I flickered in and out of sleep all night, occasionally dozing off for a few minutes, only to jerk awake again. I lay still, wrapping my arms around myself and trying to fall back asleep again, but sleep refused to come. I wanted to take a shower. I could still feel his lips on my neck, my chest. His hands, sliding across my skin, unchecked, uninvited...

I felt sick, and I knew that I couldn't lie still any longer. I rolled onto my side and checked my phone for the time. Quarter to six – early enough at last to get up. It was already light outside, but there wouldn't be too many people around yet. I wriggled out from under my blankets and climbed down from the loft above the truck cab. Dad was still asleep, stretched out on the narrow bed behind the seats. Tradition dictated that he slept there. Mum and I had always shared the loft, and Pete had slept on a stretcher in the horse area.

Pete.

I swallowed past the lump that rose in my throat. I missed my brother. If he'd been here, I could've told him what happened last night. He'd have done something about it. I couldn't tell Dad – he'd go ballistic. He'd already made enough of a scene yesterday at the practice fence; the last thing I needed was round two. Pete would've been discreet, but Dad would try to lodge some kind of formal complaint and everything would become public knowledge. My word versus Connor's, and what could I say he'd done, really? He'd stopped when I told him to. Not right away, but he'd stopped.

I wished he'd never started. I wished I'd never given him the chance.

Dad was still sleeping when I slipped out of the truck, dressed and showered, with only one thing on my mind.

Go see the ponies.

They'd make me feel better. I could put my arms around Buck's neck, and let Skip blow bubbles in my hair, and scratch Forbes behind his ears the way he liked best, and know that some things were still the same. I stepped down onto the dewy grass and pushed the door carefully shut behind me. The latch clicked, but I didn't move. My feet were frozen to the ground and I felt the blood chill in my veins, the lingering warmth of the hot shower disappearing fast at the sight of the word scrawled in large black letters on the side of our truck.

SLUT.

It wasn't even true. Couldn't have been further from the truth, in fact. My head pounded and I broke out in a fresh layer of sweat, my hands clammy, my skin prickling, all the hairs on my arms standing on end. A small corner of my brain that wasn't engaged in panicking was focused enough to wonder who'd written it, but there was really only one option.

Wasn't there?

Hoofbeats thudded on the grass nearby, and a horse whinnied, and someone told it to shut up and behave. I moved quickly, stepping closer to our truck to try and block the incriminating word from anyone else's view. The rider passed by, and I stood close and stared at the black paint, tears stinging my eyes. Why did people have to be so mean? Couldn't they just leave me alone?

Didn't they know that life was already hard enough?

I reached out with a finger and touched the paint, wondering whether it had dried yet. My heart lifted as it smeared under my touch, leaving a black mark on my finger. Not paint, I realised, but boot polish. I could smell it now, and I started rubbing harder at it, using the side of my hand. It smeared, but I could still read it. I rubbed my hands in the wet grass, then scrubbed again at the boot polish, trying to remove the evidence.

It was going to take more than water. I gathered my nerve and slipped back into the truck, then started searching under the sink for something a little stronger. There was a full bottle of Spray n' Wipe under there, and I mentally praised my mother's tendencies towards obsessive cleanliness. Grabbing a sponge, I headed back for the door as Dad rolled over and opened his eyes.

"Morning." He glanced at the clock on the dashboard and frowned. "You're up early."

"Early bird gets the worm." I was right at the door now, holding the bottle of Spray n' Wipe behind my back so he wouldn't see it, wouldn't ask what I was doing. "I'm just going to check on the boys, give them a biscuit of hay each."

"Okay." Dad propped himself up on his elbow and rubbed his eyes. "I'll get up in a minute, make us something to eat."

"No rush," I told him. Breakfast was the furthest thing from my mind right now. "Take your time." And I slipped outside again before he could say anything else.

I knew that I had to hurry. I sprayed liberal amounts of cleaning product on the boot polish, which was all smudgy now but still stubbornly readable, then started scrubbing with the course side of the sponge, designed to get grease off non-stick pans. I rubbed furiously at the side of the truck, hoping Dad couldn't hear it from inside.

Moments later, I stepped back and surveyed my work critically. You could tell that something was amiss – there was a dark smudge on the side of our truck that definitely wasn't supposed to be there – but even the wildest imagination would never be able to tell what it had said.

SLUT.

The word wouldn't stop whirling around in my head, jabbing at me with sharp fingers, making my head ache and my stomach clench.

I am not.

Then why did it say you are?

I threw the sponge underneath the truck, wishing I knew.

Instead of getting better, the day only got worse. I fed the ponies, mucked out their yards and removed their leg wraps, then started plaiting Forbes's mane. Etiquette dictated that the ponies were plaited for the final round of a Championship, and while not everyone subscribed to that tradition, I knew that Dad would expect me to have done it. My plaits still weren't as good as our former groom Lucy's had been, but I'd been practicing at home, and could manage to get them looking halfway decent.

Dad turned up just as I was sewing the last one in.

"There you are. Wondered when you were coming for breakfast."

I slid the needle through the bottom of the plait and tucked it up into the base of Forbes's mane. "Almost done."

"Plaits look good."

"Thanks." I felt a warm glow of satisfaction as I pulled the needle through the tight plait, then sewed downwards again, pulling the string tight to check the tension. Tuck the plait under again, stitch back up, and then back down again. Once more in each direction for good luck, then I pulled out the small scissors from my apron and snipped off the thread.

Lowering my aching arms, I surveyed my work proudly as Dad walked around behind Forbes and ran a hand over his hindquarters.

"No lasting lameness from yesterday then?" he asked casually, just as Forbes laid back his ears and lifted his hind leg in warning.

My heart sank like a stone as I realised that I'd completely forgotten about my pony banging his stifle on the jump yesterday. I hadn't even bothered to check whether he was walking freely before I'd started plaiting him. Even before I had to admit that to my father, before I clipped a lead rope onto Forbes's halter and stripped his rug off and led him out of his yard, before I trotted him up under my Dad's watchful eye, I just knew that he'd be lame.

And I was right.

Dad went to scratch Forbes from his class while I snipped the plaits out of his mane. Almost an hour to put them in, and now only a matter of minutes to take them all out. I threw a stable rug back over the glossy dark bay pony and rubbed his ears, then went to check on the other two. Skip was his usual cheerful self, nuzzling me in his friendly way as I ran my hands down his legs and massaged his back and hindquarters, checking for any flinching or muscle tension. Finally reassuring myself that there was nothing wrong with him, at least, I moved on to Buck.

"How're you doing this morning, old man?" Buck turned towards me and blinked slowly, as though he was only half-awake. I stepped in close and started unbuckling his neck rug, and he rubbed his cheek on my shoulder, though not as forcefully as usual. Sometimes I had to grab onto the railing to prevent being pushed right over when he took it into his head to rub on me. I stripped Buck's rugs off and looked at him with a critical eye. You'd never know that he was almost nineteen, except…

I ran my hands over his sides, looking at the way his belly was tucked up, showing a ridge below his ribcage that wasn't usually there, and at the hollowness of his flanks. I checked his water bucket to see if he'd been drinking properly, remembering that my former pony Springbok used to get tucked up like this when he got dehydrated. Buck hadn't drunk a lot of water overnight, but the bucket wasn't brimful either, so he must've had some. I stood back and surveyed him critically, worried. We always added electrolytes to the ponies' water buckets when we were away competing, but I couldn't remember whether I'd done it last night or not.

I threw a rug back over my pony. "I'll go see if Dad's got electrolyte paste in the truck," I told Buck. He wouldn't be competing today anyway, as I'd decided to give him the rest of the weekend off, but I couldn't have him standing around dehydrated. I leaned down to give him a kiss, and had to smile at the shavings stuck to his muzzle. "What've you been getting up to?"

I brushed at the shavings, then frowned as they stuck to my hand. Wiping my hand on my jeans, I looked more closely. His short coughing fit from last night came back to me, sucker-punching me in the gut, and I realised that his nose was running with a thick discharge.

Oh no.

This was not good. Buck was clearly sick, and I just hoped that it was a cold, and not something more sinister. I glanced up at the sound of footsteps, and saw Dad approaching.

"Ready for your breakfast?"

"Not yet." I bit my lip, then told my father the bad news. "I think you need to call the vet."

"Talk about your overreaction. Calling the vet out for a pony with a mild cold?"

"You know what they say about people with too much money."

"They shouldn't have the pony here if it's got a cold," someone else said. "Colds are highly contagious, and we're only a month out from Horse of the Year."

I ignored them as best I could, walking the course carefully behind the group of riders ahead of me. They had jackets slung over their arms and whips slapping against their boots as they strode out the combinations, talking in loud voices and not caring whether I heard them. I kept my steps deliberately slow, maintaining distance between us, walking unnecessarily precise lines and doing my best to focus only on the course ahead of me.

Skip was waiting outside the ring with my father, fit as a fiddle and ready to go. Buck had been moved to a yard on the end of the row for the rest of the show, a half-hearted quarantine that was making him even more depressed. A local vet had come and taken his temperature, confirmed that it was slightly elevated, given him electrolytes and a dose of Bute, and told us that we had nothing much to worry about. I'd hovered nearby, watching the vet's calm, precise movements. I still harboured a desire to be a vet myself one day, but the dream seemed more unattainable the more I sought after it. It took four hard years of study, and that was only if you got into vet school in the first place. I knew that the statistics weren't good. There was only one university in New Zealand that offered a veterinary degree. Hundreds applied, but only the top sixty got through the preliminary examinations. And then even if you did manage to pass all four years of the degree and make it onto the vet register, you still had to convince people to trust you with their animals' health. I wanted to be a large animal vet, but convincing anyone that I was competent to look after their horses seemed like it would be an impossible feat.

I paced out the distance from the grey oxer to the red vertical, then stopped and looked behind me at the subtle curve between the two jumps, memorising it. Too late, I realised that there was someone on my heels that I really didn't want to talk to.

Anna stopped next to me at the base of the red jump. Her blonde hair was tucked tightly into a hairnet under her helmet, and her grey pinstripe jacket sat elegantly on her slender shoulders.

"I've got a message for you," she said, her blue eyes meeting mine. "From Connor."

I stepped away, walking around to the other side of the jump. "I don't want to hear it."

Anna met me on the other side, one haughty eyebrow lifted. "Well I think you should."

I clenched my jaw. "Anything that Connor has to say to me, he can say to my face." I put as much conviction into my voice as I could, but inside I was quailing. Coming face-to-face with Connor was the last thing I wanted to happen today, if only because I knew I didn't have the strength to punch him in the face as hard as he deserved. "Or maybe he could just leave another note on the side of my truck."

Anna frowned, looking like she had no idea what I was talking about, then shook off her confusion. "Whatever. He just said to tell you that he's got someone else looking at Star, so you won't be able to compete her this afternoon."

She strode away without waiting for a response, leaving me alone in the middle of the course, wanting nothing more than for this day to be over already.

I rode badly in the warm-up, distracted by the sight of Connor standing next to the practice jump as his sister Grace schooled Summertime over it. His voice rang out as he reminded her to sit up and balance.

"Use your legs, they're not painted on!"

I could hear other riders chuckling at his jokes, and saw Grace grinning at her brother. I avoided looking at him, trying to focus on my pony, but when I cantered Skip down to the vertical, Connor was still standing next to it. I was three strides away when he took a step towards the jump and rested a hand on the pole, distracting me. I checked Skip hard, and he threw up his head and shortened his stride. We'd been coming in on the perfect distance, and now I'd flubbed it. I kicked on, and my pony put in a huge effort, but he rattled the rail, which tumbled to the ground.

I gave Skip an apologetic pat as I cantered on, glancing over at the jump as we made the turn. Anna had been following me to the jump, and had been forced to circle when Skip had knocked it. She shot me a dirty look as she brought her pony Saxon back to a trot, but I was distracted by the sight of Connor and my dad putting the rail back up. Together. One on each end of the rail, chatting and smiling like they were friends. Connor turned and caught my eye, smirking. He knew I hadn't told my dad anything – he'd been banking on it. I almost wished I had, if only to wipe that look off his face, but I couldn't bring myself to do it. The last thing I needed was to have any more attention drawn to me.

Anna cleared the rebuilt jump on Saxon, and I took Skip around for another attempt. I could feel Connor's eyes on me as I rode down to it, and my hands went tight and clammy on the reins. Skip tossed his head again, slowing down so much that he almost broke into a trot, and I had to really push him on to make it to the jump. He jumped awkwardly, his ears pinned back, and I heard my father snap at me as he lifted the rail back up.

"Get it together, Susie!"

I walked Skip on a long rein, staying as far away from Dad as possible while I tried to recover my composure. Finally, Connor walked to the gate with Grace, who was being called into the ring. Without him staring at me, I might have a chance at getting over the practice jump, and I shortened my reins and pushed Skip back into a canter. He jumped cleanly over the oxer, and I changed the rein and brought him around for the vertical, only to find that it had been lowered to a crossrail.

Lily's father stood next to it with his arms folded, daring me to object. I said nothing as I eased Skip back to a walk while Lily trotted over the crossrail on her bay gelding Double Happy, who snapped up his knees at the base, jumping it in perfect form. Lily held a textbook perfect position in the saddle, and her father beamed proudly at her as she cantered on. He stepped closer to the practice fence, and called to Lily to come and jump it again.

I knew what he was doing, and I didn't blame him. But from the corner of my eye, I could see Dad approaching, and I knew he would quickly cotton on to the situation. I didn't need another confrontation, so moved quickly to divert him.

"Dad, can you go get my gloves from the truck?"

He frowned up at me, squinting in the bright sunlight. "You want to wear gloves, in this heat?"

I shrugged. "He keeps throwing his head."

"So stop grabbing at his mouth."

Gone were the days when everything the ponies did wrong was considered their fault – now Dad took the opposite tack, always laying the blame at my front door. Not that he was wrong, but it would've been nice to feel as though he was still on my side.

"I'm trying, okay?" I struggled to keep a lid on my temper. "Gloves will help. Bruce always tells me to wear them when I start fiddling too much with the reins."

Dad's expression changed at my use of the magical B-word. Anything that Bruce said was gospel in his mind, and he slapped me on the leg in affirmation before striding off towards our truck. Relieved to have him out of my hair, I rode Skip towards the ring, watching as Summertime sailed through the treble and made the turn towards the Liverpool. Summer baulked a little on the approach, Connor yelled encouragement and I heard the thwack of Grace's crop slapping down against Summer's shoulder as the pony prepared to take off. Summer flew over the jump, then belted on down to the last with Grace clinging like a limpet, left half a stride early and had to stretch to make it, but landed clear.

"All clear for Grace Campbell and Summertime," said the announcer as Connor and his parents clapped and cheered. "So they'll be back for the jump-off. Next into the ring and currently sitting in third place overall is Lily Christianson, riding Westbrook Double Happy." Lily trotted into the ring and gave Grace a high five as they passed each other. Double Happy pricked his ears and looked around the course with interest as the bell rang, and Lily started her course.

"I still can't believe that she only started riding two years ago," a woman on the sidelines gushed. "You must be so proud of her."

The blonde woman standing next to her smiled, her eyes still fixed on Lily as she responded. "Oh we are! As soon as she started taking lessons we realised she was a natural, and when Lil decides to do something, she goes all out. We've been lucky, too, to find such wonderful ponies for her to learn on," she added, sucking in a breath as Lily misjudged her take-off spot to the grey vertical. But Double Happy was a pro, tucking his forelegs up quickly to avoid taking the rail and scraping over cleanly. "Happ is just wonderful, he's been absolutely perfect for her to learn on."

"Have you put her name down for the team going to Ireland in May?" the woman asked, and Lily's mother nodded.

"Of course, Lily's so excited about the prospect. We've got our fingers tightly crossed!"

I frowned as I watched Happ jumped tidily through the double, Lily still posing perfectly on his back. She looked good, but if she'd only started riding two years ago, how could she realistically have enough experience to compete in a big team competition on borrowed horses? It was only Happ's honest nature and impeccable schooling that was getting her around the course clear today. They came down to the treble combination, and Happ steadied himself as he approached the line of fences, trying to get a read on the question. Lily misunderstood his intentions and spurred him on, thinking he was baulking. Obediently, the pony sped up, reaching the first fence with too much pace, and I sucked in a sharp breath. But he made it over the first fence cleanly, and Lily at least had the good sense to give him his head and let him get out of trouble. He was incredible and managed, somehow, to jump through clear.

Lily's mother started bleating on about how brave her daughter was, instead of praising the pony for his exceptional ability to save her child's skin, so I turned Skip and rode away. I was sure my parents had been equally eager to gloat about me when I was younger, but it didn't make it any less nauseating to listen to.

I took Skip over the vertical once more as Anna jogged Saxon to the gate for her round. Dad returned with my gloves, and I thanked him as I pulled them on. I actually hated riding in gloves, but it was a bit late to change my mind now.

Lily was patting her pony enthusiastically as she rode out of the ring. "And that's all clear for Lily Christianson. We have two riders left to jump, and they both need to go clear to stay in the running for the overall Championship," the announcer said gleefully. "The points are very tight at the top of the table, and there is no margin for error today."

Great. I declined Dad's suggestion that I jump one more practice fence, and went to the gate and watched Anna go. Saxon jumped the first half of the course well, but he slipped on the way to the treble and had the first rail down.

"That's her out of it," Dad said, sounding annoyingly smug. "Now, remember. You have to go clear, and you have to finish first or second in the jump-off to get the title. Well, you can manage third if Lily doesn't place above you, but if she beats you then you'll drop down to second…"

I did my best to tune him out as Anna completed the course. She didn't have any more faults, but she looked bitterly disappointed as she cantered through the finish flags, knowing that her last shot at the title was gone.

"And now we have our final rider on course," came the call, startling Skip sideways as we trotted past the speaker. "Susannah Andrews and Skybeau, currently at the top of the table by a whisker, and needing a clear round within the time to progress to the jump off."

I took a breath, squeezed Skip up into a canter, and let everything else fade out. No crowd. No pressure. Nothing except the pony beneath me, the rhythm of his strides as he cantered across the hard ground.

One, two, three.

Skip's breaths. The arch of his neck as he lifted his head to sight the first fence.

One, two, three.

The reins between my gloved fingers. My seat sinking into the saddle on the approach. My legs wrapping around his sides. The lightest touch of the spur.

One, two, three.

Over the white oxer, and around the corner to fence two. Skip's legs tucked up tight beneath us as he cleared it. The gentle thud as we landed.

One, two, three.

Someone shouted, and there was a clatter of poles at the practice fence. People all around us started moving, turning away, their attention distracted by whatever was going on outside of the ring. Skip slowed down slightly and I kicked him on. Too hard. He launched forward and flung himself into the air over the rustic oxer, but hit the back rail hard on the way down.

I shouldn't have done it – it's a cardinal rule of show jumping that you don't look back. You should never look back. But I had to know whether the rail had fallen, whether my chance was gone. So I turned my head, only for a moment. Just to check.

The rail was still sitting in its cups. But my relief was short-lived as I looked back to where we were headed and realised that Skip had locked onto the blue vertical – but it was the wrong fence. I pulled him out sharply, and he flung his head up, startled. Fence five, a wide triple bar, was right in front of us and at a nearly impossible angle. For a second, I wondered whether I should just pull out and circle, conceding four faults for crossing my tracks, but not asking my pony to do the impossible. But I didn't. I had to commit to the fence, or Dad would give me hell all the way home. So I sat down harder and pushed Skip on, sure that he could do it if he only tried hard enough.

Skip shot forward, snatching at the bit, his head high in the air. Too late, I realised that we wouldn't make it. Too late, I realised that I'd asked too much of my gallant pony.

Too late.

Skip knew, moments before I did, that I was asking him to do the impossible. He started to add a stride, then gave up and slammed on the brakes. His forelegs collided with the front of the jump, and poles rained down as the wings knocked into each other, demolishing the entire fence.

The buzzer sounded, and I backed Skip slowly out of the wreckage and gave him an apologetic pat, my heart sinking. He jogged nervously on the spot, sweating hard, his eyes rolling.

"I'm sorry mate," I murmured to him. "That was entirely my fault. I'm so sorry."

I circled him, continuing to rub his neck reassuringly as he slowed to a walk, starting to relax a little. I leaned against his neck and put an arm around him, giving him a cuddle. He tucked his nose in and let out a deep breath, and I reached forward and rubbed behind his ears, talking softly to him the whole time.

The bell rang again, and I straightened up and shortened my reins. Skip danced underneath me, his nerves returning, and I took a deep breath of my own. Looked towards the jump, and saw Connor.

He was moonlighting as a ring steward and had helped them to reset the fence. Now he was walking back into the centre of the ring alongside the course designer. Watching me. He smirked as he caught my eye, and my insides clenched up reflexively.

Ignore him. I picked up a canter, and rode Skip down to the triple bar, focusing hard on getting a better distance this time. My pony was still unsure, swerving slightly on the approach, but I got him to the base and this time he cleared the jump.

"Good boy," I told him as we cantered around the corner. We were out of the running now, but I wanted Skip to regain his confidence over a couple good fences before I took him out of the ring.

I should've quit while I was ahead. Skip was still rattled, and he hit the planks, spooked at the wall, and backed off so much at the treble that it was all I could do to keep him cantering through it. He scraped over all three jumps, but he wasn't happy about it, and I felt terrible as I cantered through the flags, knowing that we'd just put in the worst performance of our career.

Dad met me at the gate, so angry that he could barely look at me. He just walked alongside as I rode back towards the truck, his only concession being to pat Skip briefly on the neck, recognising that it wasn't the pony's fault that we'd had such a disastrous round. He stayed quiet while I untacked Skip and hosed him down, took out his studs and gave him a feed. My father didn't say anything as I bandaged the other ponies' legs and got them ready to travel, ignoring me as much as he could while he mucked out and tidied the yards, packed up our buckets and emptied our haynets.

He saved his remonstrations until we were ready to go, with the ponies on board and the truck packed tight. He climbed up into the cab and turned the key, waiting for the glow light to go off before he started the diesel engine. I rolled down the passenger window to let some fresh air into the hot cab as the loudspeaker blared out over the show grounds, giving the final results after the jump off. Lily had won. Dad snorted and started the engine, drowning out the announcement of the remaining placings. I heard cheering as Lily rode into the ring, and Dad finally spoke.

"That should've been you."

I flinched as he finally spoke, and dared to look in his direction, but he was staring straight ahead.

"What were you thinking?"

"I lost focus, that's all," I muttered.

"That's *all?*" He took a breath, preparing to continue, but I cut him off.

"Dad, don't. I know, okay? I *know* that I screwed up. I don't need you to tell me everything I did wrong, because I *know*. I got distracted. I looked back. I made my poor pony jump off stupid angles. I missed distances. I'm lucky Skip didn't throw me into the jumps in disgust, and I would've deserved it if he had." I racked my brains for more things that Dad might say, wanting to say them out loud before he could. "I've wasted your time and your money and I'm sorry, okay?"

Dad looked at me as he drove slowly out of the show grounds, then nodded, accepting my apology.

I rested my head back into the corner of the cab and closed my eyes, trying to forget. Dad turned the radio on, filling the cab with upbeat pop music.

…'cause I am a champion, and you're gonna hear me…

I flinched, and Dad hit a button, changing the radio station. I closed my eyes as the new lyrics swirled around me, trying to ignore the clenching in my stomach.

Who do you think you are? Running 'round, leaving scars…

This song was even worse than the last one. I tried to refocus my thoughts, tried to concentrate on the round I'd just jumped, mercilessly picking apart my own performance as I strove desperately to ignore the other voice in my head. The one that didn't care about how badly Skip had jumped, because it was still too busy freaking out about last night.

But it wouldn't be silenced.

I wish I had missed the first time that we kissed…

I wished I could go back, could rewind the clock three days, could do this entire weekend over again. There were so many things I would've done differently. And never striking up a conversation with Connor in the first place was right there at the top of the list.

But you knew, the voice inside me said. *You knew who he was, and what he was like. You knew better, but you couldn't help being flattered by the attention. You thought maybe you were different, not like the other girls. You thought maybe he really truly liked you.* The voice gave a mocking laugh. *But why would he?*

I shook my head, trying to make the voice shut up. I opened my eyes again and stared out at the rolling brown hills on either side of us, trying really hard not to let my father see me cry.

6

FIGHT OR FLIGHT

It was almost a relief to be back at school on Tuesday. Nobody there knew anything about what had gone on at Nationals – the handful of other girls in my year who were riders weren't competitive enough to compete at the same shows as I did. They rode at a local riding school, borrowing ponies for Pony Club, still desperately trying to talk their parents into purchasing their own. Susannah Andrews, with her string of show jumpers and obsessively competitive parents, was outside of their realm of experience, and they seemed to want to keep it that way.

I sat through our introduction assembly, barely listening as the Headmistress and her offsiders prattled on about applying ourselves and being the best we could be, while all around me girls fidgeted and whispered and compared nail polish and tan lines. I pretended to listen, my thoughts still at home where Buck was grazing in a paddock alongside my other two ponies. I hoped he was okay.

He hadn't had another coughing episode until we got home, but he'd developed a murky discharge from one nostril that was concerning enough for Dad to call our local vet clinic for a second opinion. Much to Dad's disappointment, our usual vet Donald was on a six month sabbatical. Dad liked Donald, because he'd always listen carefully to my father as though he knew what he was talking about, and always pretended to take his opinion into account. He also always prescribed some form of medication, even if it was one of the many occasions when Dad had called him in for next to no reason. I wasn't sure whether it was to make Dad feel like he'd got his money's worth or because he just wanted to milk us for all we were worth. Probably both. I was fairly certain that Donald could've bought himself a holiday house with the money that Dad had pumped into his practice over the years, but at least he knew how to keep my father placated.

The new vet, Lesley, didn't have the same finesse. She was a small, youngish woman with a thick mane of auburn hair and a firm handshake. Dad had immediately tried to tell her how to do her job, so she'd promptly ignored him, turning her back on him to examine Buck, even shushing him while she'd listened to my pony's heartbeat. It would've been funny if it hadn't made Dad so difficult. She'd concurred that Buck appeared to have contracted a mild cold, but as he wasn't running a fever, she simply prescribed isolation and rest for a few days until he was back to himself. When Dad had told her that it was midsummer and a ridiculous time for anyone to get a cold, she had simply smiled at him and said that he was probably right. She'd swabbed a small amount of nasal discharge but had refused to give us any antibiotics in the absence of stronger symptoms.

Dad had been livid at what he interpreted as a refusal to adequately medicate Buck, and Lesley's suggestion to feed the pony crushed garlic in a bran mash "if you must give him something" had met with further anger, which she'd continued to seem utterly oblivious to. Eventually she'd offered to inject Buck with a placebo if it would make Dad feel better, and he'd stormed out of the barn. Lesley had just winked at me as she snapped her kit shut, and told me to ring her if anything changed.

People around me started to move, and I realised that assembly was finally done. I checked the timetable that I'd downloaded last night and headed towards my new classroom, stopping off at the toilets on the way. There was a crush of girls in there, peering at themselves in the mirror and applying makeup, telling each other to hurry up or they'd be late and they didn't want to get in trouble on the first day. Everyone was waiting for at least one other person, chattering non-stop as they admired each other's new hair colour or new jewellery or surreptitious tattoos that were barely hidden under ankle socks. I felt their eyes sliding across me as I blended silently into the background of their laments about the classes they'd been put into, the teachers they'd have to suffer through, the tragic loss of summer's freedom.

When I finally got access to a cubicle, I shut the door behind me and twisted the lock, then I saw something written on the back of the door that made my skin turn cold.

For a good time, call Susie.

I knew right away that it wasn't about me. Nobody here called me Susie, and it certainly wasn't my phone number underneath, but it rattled me nonetheless. I took a deep breath and pressed the heels of my hands against my eyes. *Calm down. Just breathe.* I felt like a skittish horse in a new situation, with no idea of how to react, and an overwhelming instinct to run away.

Horses have what's known as a flight instinct. Like other prey animals, their natural predisposition is to run away when they feel threatened. Unlike predators, who are far more likely to stand their ground and fight. I've always been a fighter. I come from a long line of fighters, of people who won't back down, no matter what.

And look where that's got us.

I gritted my teeth, hating the tightness in my muscles, the roiling in my stomach, the cold sweat on my skin. I wanted to run, but there was nowhere to go, and nothing to run from. But there was nothing to fight either, and nowhere to lay the blame, except at my own door. I shook my head, telling myself to put what had happened at Nationals behind me. It hadn't even been that big of a deal, that much of a terrible thing. Far worse things than that happened to other people all the time, and they could still get out of bed in the morning and function normally.

So what was wrong with me?

I heard the outer door swing open, and a woman's voice. "Everyone get to your classrooms now, come on. There's no time for lollygagging about."

Even if I hadn't instantly recognised Ms Bryant's cheerful tone, I'd have known her for the use of such a ridiculous turn of phrase as 'lollygagging'. I'd had several sessions with our guidance counsellor last year, and although I'd actually found her surprisingly easy to talk to, I froze up at the thought of her calling me back into her office this year.

I wanted to have good news for her, but nothing good seemed to have happened lately.

"Sorry I'm late! I've got a note."

I lifted my head and watched as Callie Taylor strode into our homeroom with enviable self-assurance. If there was a most popular girl award for our year, Callie would win it. Tall, blonde and beautiful, she turned heads every time she walked into a room, and she knew it. I watched her, wishing that I had a fraction of her self-confidence.

She waved a piece of blue paper at Miss Rutherford, our reluctant supervisor, then slapped it down on her desk and spun away, her glossy hair swirling around her shoulders. The note lifted into the air, caught up in Callie's wake, and slipped between Miss Rutherford's fingers as she reached for it. I watched the slip of paper flutter to the floor as Callie scanned the room, deciding where to sit. There was an empty desk next to her best friend Esther Blake, sitting a couple of rows back, but Callie sat down at the empty desk next to me instead.

Miss Rutherford scowled as she used a long fingernail to lift the paper from the floor, and the low murmur of conversation picked up in volume again. Callie crossed her legs and turned in her chair to face me with a friendly smile.

"Hi Susannah. How was your summer?"

"Um, good." I tried to play it cool, as though she talked to me all the time, while my heart hammered in my chest in astonishment at being singled out for her attention. "How was yours?"

"Brilliant. Way better than being here." She rolled her eyes, lifting her hand to inspect her manicured fingernails. "I can't believe we're back for another year of torture."

Over her shoulder, I could see Esther staring pitifully at Callie's back. Last year they'd been practically joined at the hip, and now Callie was treating her as though she didn't exist. I wondered what had happened, and who had been at fault.

Callie slid her chair closer to me and leaned over to look at my timetable. "Are you taking Econ again this year?"

I shook my head. "No. I was trying to avoid *her*," I explained, nodding towards Miss Rutherford, who was tapping away at her laptop and ignoring the class.

Callie laughed. "Me too. I guess we both failed."

"I guess so."

The bell rang, drowning out whatever Callie said next. She pulled a face, looking personally affronted that she'd been interrupted, then swiped my timetable off my desk as she stood up and perused it.

"We're in the same English class for second period," she declared, sounding pleased. "Thank God I'll have *someone* to talk to."

I stood up as well as Esther walked out of the room with her head down. Callie didn't even glance in her direction.

By the end of the day, I'd sat with Callie in English and History, had eaten lunch with her and her friends, and spent our free study period in the library listening to her stories of skiing in Aspen over the New Year.

"It was gorgeous. Have you been?"

I shook my head. "I'm not much of a skier."

"You're missing out," Callie said confidently. "Although I wish we could've gone a week later. It sucked missing New Year's Eve here. What'd you do for it?"

"Um." I tried to think of something cooler to say than *sat at home watching movies with my mum.* "Not much."

Callie raised a carefully plucked eyebrow. "You didn't go out?"

"No. I don't go out much during the show season." Or during the off season, but I didn't say that out loud.

A vague look of confusion flickered across Callie's face for a moment, then it cleared again. "Oh yeah, you ride horses or something, right?"

"Yeah."

"That's cool. I took riding lessons when I was younger, but I didn't really like it." She smiled at me, and I smiled half-heartedly back. "Mum was desperate to buy me a pony, and we tried one out, but I fell off it and lost interest after that."

I couldn't think of what to say. "Right." I switched my attention to the blank sheet of paper in front of me. "Could this assignment be any more vague?" I asked her. "Write a poem. How long does it have to be? Does it have to rhyme?"

Callie shrugged. "Who cares? It's not worth any credits. Just make something up. Write a few words backwards or something. Are you any good?"

I frowned. "At writing poetry?"

"Duh, no. At riding horses."

"Oh. Um, I'm okay."

I wondered if saying that I came seventh at Nationals would sound impressive to her uninformed ears, or whether it would sound as pathetic to her as it did to me. Dad had looked it up online as we'd travelled home on the ferry. He hadn't said anything, just showed me the results on his phone, as if I'd needed reminding that I'd screwed up.

The blank sheet of paper lay in front of me, mocking me. I

wondered if I could write a poem about my ponies. I thought about Buck's glossy dark coat, Skip's whiskery nose, Forbes's curved ears. But I couldn't get any words to flow. I scratched my pen against the corner of the page in meaningless swirls, searching for inspiration.

"Is this you?"

"Huh?" I turned towards Callie, who was looking at a video on her phone. She tilted it towards me, and I saw footage of Buck flying over a jump in last year's Pony of the Year class. She must have Googled my name, and found the clip on YouTube. "Oh. Yeah."

"Those jumps are big."

I nodded, relieved that she sounded impressed.

"Did you win?"

I shook my head. "Not quite. I came second."

"Bummer. That's still good though."

Callie lost interest in Buck, turning her phone's screen dark as my pony headed down to the treble in the middle of the ring. He disappeared, and I wondered how he was doing at home. I'd taken Lesley's advice to keep him separated from the other two, but Buck hated being on his own. He'd whinnied to them all night from his isolation paddock, and they'd whinnied back from the barn until Dad had made me go out and move the other two into a nearby paddock overnight so they could at least see one another. That had quieted Buck for now, but there wasn't much grass in any of the paddocks, so we'd had to supplement them all with hay. Fortunately we'd had our winter hay supply delivered just before Nationals, but Dad wasn't happy about having to feed out over summer.

"So you know how it's Valentine's Day this weekend?" It was Callie's turn to change the subject, and I looked back over at her.

"Is it?"

She rolled her eyes at me. "Duh. Obviously. I'm going to make Mum let me have a party, since I didn't get to have people over for New Year's. What d'you think?"

"Sure. Sounds good," I responded vaguely.

"You'll come, right?"

"Uh, sure," I said. "Wait, this weekend?" She nodded, and I shook my head reluctantly. "I can't. I've got Taihape."

"Taihape?" she repeated, making it sound like a dirty word. "What's in Taihape, other than gumboots?"

"Show jumping."

"Oh." She pursed her lips and knotted her eyebrows together. "You really are into this horse thing, aren't you?"

"Yeah." For the first time in my life, I was wondering what it would be like if I wasn't. What if I could ride *and* have a social life? I still wasn't convinced that I wanted to go to Callie's party, but it was nice to have the option.

"Well, that's too bad. I was looking forward to getting you all dolled up for it." She tilted her head and looked at me critically. "You really should wear more makeup. You're really pretty, you know."

You're so pretty. I made myself smile, knowing she meant it as a compliment. Trying to push Connor's voice out of my head. "Thanks."

"I mean it," she said, tucking her hair behind one ear. A diamond stud glittered in her earlobe. "You're wasting your God given talents. You know what they say – if you've got it, flaunt it!" Callie turned to me with a sultry expression and fluttered her eyelashes, then pouted again. "*Why* did we have to get stuck at a stupid all girls' school?"

7

MOVE YOUR FEET

The sun was lowering over the Taihape show grounds as I stepped out of our truck on Saturday evening. My jandals crunched on the dry grass, and the sprinklers that were hissing water across the jumping rings were barely making a difference to the rock hard ground.

Dad straightened up from his crouch by the truck's water tank and looked at me. "Where are you off to?"

"Katy's truck. I'm having dinner with them. I told you."

"Oh, right."

I felt bad about leaving him alone, but Katy had already told me that her mum was spending the evening with her friends, so I couldn't ask him to join us. If he tried a little harder to make friends of his own, maybe he wouldn't be in this position. I pushed away that uncharitable thought and gave him a quick wave as I started to walk away.

"Are the ponies fed?"

"Yes."

"Did you wrap Skip's legs?"

I stopped and looked back at him. "Yes. And Forbes's as well, and they've got hay, and water, and I've skipped out. Anything else?"

"Did you clean your tack?" He was really grasping at straws now.

"I'll do it in the morning," I assured him.

"Don't be too late. Forbes is on first thing."

"I know. I won't," I called back as I started walking again. "Besides,

Katy's in the same class and she's first to go. It's not going to be a late night."

I walked down the line of trucks, enjoying the warm evening air on my bare arms and legs. It had been a hot day, but my ponies had jumped well. Skip had won the metre-twenty speed, and Forbes had jumped double clear in the metre ten that afternoon, making up for his misbehaviour at Nationals. I saw Katy's truck up ahead, and heard AJ's loud laughter emanating from it. The ramp was down, and Katy stepped down onto it with an armful of feed buckets. Her dark hair was falling out of its ponytail, and she had a dirty streak down her bare leg.

"Need any help?" I offered, eyeing up the buckets in her arms.

"Oh hey," she greeted me. "No I'm good, these are for the morning. Just trying to be prepared."

"For once in your life," AJ teased her, appearing at the back of the truck. She had her arm in a sling, reminding me of the injury that she'd sustained in a car accident on New Year's Eve. It had been a rough start to the year for her too, but she was beaming at me as though she didn't have a care in the world. "How are you always so clean?" she asked, her blue eyes scanning me from top to toe.

I blushed, shrugging. "I had a shower."

"Ah, that'd explain it. Did you hear that, Katy?"

"I heard."

"Just a little friendly suggestion from the person who has to sleep next to you tonight," AJ said casually as Katy jumped off the ramp and opened one of the side hatches with one hand, doing her best to wedge the buckets in. I went to help her.

"Thanks." Katy shoved a pile of covers that had been crammed into the small space to the side, then pushed the buckets into the gap, where they tilted precariously back towards her. "I think they'll stay there," she said optimistically.

I shot her a dubious look. "I don't."

"Aren't you Susie Sunshine today?" she asked. "Don't be such a pessimist."

"It's not pessimism, it's physics," I replied. "This little thing called gravity."

"Pfft." Katy rolled her eyes at me. "We've just gotta be quick. Shut the hatch on three. Ready? One, two, three!"

She let go of the buckets and stepped back before I could tell her that it was a really stupid idea, because even if I could get the hatch closed in time to keep the feed buckets wedged into the gap, they would all fall out the moment anyone opened it again. Katy didn't appear to have thought of that, but since I failed to shut the hatch on three, the buckets tumbled out as soon as she let go of them – just as I'd known they would – and scattered their contents across the dry grass.

AJ roared with laughter as Katy stared at me indignantly. "You didn't shut it!"

"I told you it wasn't going to work."

"It would've worked if you'd just shut it when I told you to."

"Now, now, girls. No catfights in the public arena."

The smile disappeared off my face at the sound of his voice, but Katy spun on her heel to greet Connor cheerfully.

"Not my fault if Susannah can't follow a simple instruction," she told him.

Connor looked at me, catching my eye for a brief moment before I looked away. I saw the smirk on his face as he stood silhouetted against the fading daylight.

"She's not too good at following instructions," he said smugly.

Why hadn't I taken karate lessons, or judo or something? I wanted nothing more than to wipe that look off his face, but I was powerless. Struck motionless, holding up Katy's truck hatch as she chatted with Connor, unable to move. I could feel his eyes on me, and it was making my skin crawl.

Fight or flight.

I couldn't fight him, and I couldn't leave.

Yes you can.

I took a deep breath, then another one.

Move your feet.

I let go of the hatch and it slammed shut, making everyone jump. They all looked at me, but I just turned and walked down towards the open side door, then climbed the steps into Katy's truck. It wasn't very far away, but at least I didn't have to look at Connor any more. I sat down on the sofa and put my head in my hands, trying to settle my nerves. Hating that I'd run away. Unable to face going back out there until I knew he was gone.

"Are you okay?" It was AJ, standing in the doorway and looking at me with concern in her eyes.

I pushed my hair back, relieved that I wasn't actually crying. "I'm fine. Just a bit tired."

"You sure?"

I nodded. "Honestly, I'm good."

I didn't want to talk about it. If I told her – if I told anyone – it made it real. Then she'd know, and she'd pity me. And even if I could persuade her not to tell anyone, Connor would know that she knew. I didn't want him to have the satisfaction of knowing that he'd got to me. I just wanted to be able to walk away from it all and forget it ever happened.

"Are you going to help me pick these feeds up?" Katy stuck her head around the side door and looked at me. "Since you're the reason I dropped them?"

"Gravity is the reason you dropped them," AJ reminded her on my behalf. "Pick them up yourself, you've got two arms."

Katy rolled her eyes, but I stood up. "Sorry. I'll help you."

"On three this time," she reminded me as I climbed back down the steps.

"Or you could pull those rugs out of the hatch and fold them so the buckets will actually fit," I suggested, reflexively glancing over at the spot where Connor had been standing moments earlier. He'd gone, and I let out a breath I hadn't realised I was holding.

Katy and I were scraping feeds off the ground when another male voice interrupted us. "You know, you could just mix the feeds *in* the buckets."

"Way too mainstream," Katy said, rocking back onto her heels and squinting up at Jonty, who was grinning down at us. Tess was by his side as usual, the two of them joined by an invisible thread that seemed to be getting shorter and stronger as time went on.

Tess shot me a hesitant smile, and I smiled back. We weren't exactly friends, mostly because her sister Hayley was a prime cow who delighted in making my life a misery. But Hayley hadn't been around much lately, and while it was widely rumoured that she was currently afflicted by some health problems, nobody really knew much more than that.

Or so I'd thought, anyway.

"Hey guys," AJ greeted them both, pushing herself upright from where she'd been slouched against the side of the truck. "How's it going?"

"Not bad," Jonty said, but Tess pulled a face and said "Crap" at the same time.

"Look, AJ!" Katy exclaimed. "They're having a difference of opinion! Quick, someone take a photo before the moment's lost."

Tess blushed, but Jonty just grinned at Katy and retaliated by putting a foot under the feed bucket in her hands and flipping it upside down, spilling the contents back onto the scorched dirt.

"Hey! Uncalled for!"

"Totally called for," Jonty contradicted her. "Didn't your mother ever tell you that if you can't say something nice, don't say anything at all?"

"Nobody told *my* mother that," Tess grumbled, picking her way past Katy's pile of spilled feed on her way towards AJ. "She's been a total nightmare today."

AJ looked sympathetic. "I heard."

Tess huffed out a breath. "I think *everyone* heard."

She wasn't wrong. Tess had taken three rails in the metre twenty that morning, and her mother had given her an earful about it all the way from the gate back to their truck, and then for another several minutes after that until Jonty had intervened and separated them. I couldn't really blame her for sticking to him like glue, since he seemed to be the only one who had her back against her mother, whose increasingly frequent tirades against her daughter were making my dad look like Father of the Year.

"How's Hayley?" AJ asked quietly as I scooped up another handful of feed and dumped it into the blue bucket at my side. I wasn't trying to eavesdrop, but although Tess spoke softly, she was standing close enough to me that her voice was clearly audible.

"She's okay. Last round of radiation coming up, then it's a wait and see to find out if it's worked, or whether they'll have to try and operate. They're hoping they won't, because brain surgery's always risky, but we won't know anything for a while yet."

I stared at the flakes of cracked maize scattered amongst the short grass at my feet, my head whirling. I'd known something was up with Hayley, because she'd had a seizure at a show a few weeks ago and then disappeared off the circuit, but I hadn't had any idea that it was *that* serious. And AJ didn't react the way I had, because obviously she knew – had probably known all along. I glanced up at Katy, who was chatting with Jonty as he helped her scoop up the feed he'd spilled. He knew, of course, and I could almost guarantee that what AJ knew, Katy knew too. I felt so out of the loop, and wondered why nobody had told me.

You didn't ask.

I had to face the fact that while I was friendly with Katy and AJ, their tolerance for me didn't necessarily extend to their other friends. Jonty was nice to everyone, but Tess was still standoffish, and I got a strong sense that she didn't trust me.

"Fingers crossed, eh?"

I heard Tess sigh. "Yeah, here's hoping. Hayley's convinced that it's working and she'll be riding again in no time."

"That's good," AJ replied. "Power of positive thinking and all."

"Well, you know Hayley," Tess said. "She doesn't really take defeat too well."

"I think you got it all," Katy said, stopping in front of me and casting a long shadow across the space between us.

I straightened up, feeling my left knee click the way it always had since my pony had rammed it into a jump stand when I was nine. I looked at AJ's arm in its sling, at the scar on Jonty's hand, the graze on Katy's elbow and the scattered pimples on Tess's chin, and wondered if anyone made it through life unscathed.

"So have you put your name forward for Ireland yet?" Katy asked me later as we sprawled out in her truck, eating pizza out of takeaway boxes.

"Yeah, Dad sent the application in a couple of days ago," I told her. "You?"

"Mmhmm." Katy picked a mushroom off the piece of pizza in her hand and flicked it back into the box, then took a small bite. "Signed, sealed and delivered. Well, emailed."

"Ugh, I'm so jealous," AJ grumbled.

None of us said anything. Even without her injury, AJ didn't have the experience or competition record to be in the running for a team event like that. I would've liked to have her on the team though, I realised. Of all the people in the truck, she was the one I liked the most.

"I'm not," Tess said firmly, tossing a crust back into the pizza box and picking up another slice. "You're welcome to it."

"You just don't want to go because you wouldn't be able to take Jonty with you," Katy teased her. "You'd have to spend more than twelve hours apart." She gave a dramatic gasp and clutched at her chest. "Heaven forbid."

"Don't be jealous, Katy," Jonty told her, stretching his legs out in front of him and scratching the bottom of one foot with his opposite toe. "Just because Tess got in first."

Katy spluttered. "Hah! Not if you were the last person on earth."

"Hey now," Tess retorted, indignant on her boyfriend's behalf, and he turned and grinned at her.

"At least someone loves me."

Katy gagged and looked at me, bringing the subject back to her original topic. "So anyway, I've been asking around about who else has put their names forward, and I reckon you and I are guaranteed the Junior spots."

AJ snorted, but Katy ignored her.

"That'd be nice," I said cautiously. "Better not get ahead of ourselves though."

Katy waved a hand dismissively. "You have to be under sixteen, so that wipes out the likes of Anna, although I heard she's gunning for an Intermediate spot, which she'll probably get because her family's loaded and they've been putting her forward for teams since she was about twelve." Katy wiped melted cheese off her chin and took another small bite of her pizza. "But in the Juniors, there's pretty slim pickings. Who else are they gonna take? Grace Campbell's way too feeble, and Emmalee Wilkinson is too much of a midget. Besides, she's even more ineffectual than Grace. She only gets round because that pony she's got is a complete rock star."

She had a point, but she'd forgotten someone. "Lily Christianson won big at Nationals," I pointed out. "And she won the Grand Prix at Ride the Rhythm last month."

Katy pulled a face. "Only because we didn't go," she said, making AJ roll her eyes. "And if they put that kid in the team, in her first – *first* – season of show jumping, then I'd pull out. I'm not even kidding."

"She's a good rider," Tess said. I stopped chewing and looked at her, unsure whether she was playing devil's advocate, or if she actually thought Lily was a better choice for the team than me or Katy.

"She's good at posing in the saddle," Katy corrected her, unfazed by Tess's rebuttal. "She's got a half-decent eye for a stride, I'll give her that much, but everything she's ever ridden is a total pushbutton ride. Chuck her on Misty and see how she gets on," she suggested with a glint in her eye, and Tess grinned and shook her head.

"He'd probably kill her."

"Exactly."

Tess looked over at me, and I felt like I could read her mind. *Your ponies are pushbutton rides too.* I spoke before she could.

"Another reason I'm glad we bought Forbes," I said. "He's given me a chance to prove that I can ride more than just easy ponies."

"Exactly," Katy nodded. "And you rode Squib that time, which proves you're pretty much up for anything."

AJ immediately intervened in her pony's defence, and Jonty backed her up as Katy threw her hands up in surrender.

"Fine, Squib's perfect and wonderful and sublime, whatever," she said deferentially. "The delusion is real." She was grinning though, and ducked as AJ threw a piece of mushroom at her head.

"I heard that Stacey Winchester put her name forward," Tess said, cutting through their squabbling. Everyone stopped talking and stared at her in surprise.

"Seriously? Speaking of delusional. And she's too old."

"She wants to go Intermediate," Tess clarified, making Katy snort again. "Her dad was talking to Mum earlier. He kept going on about them having family over in the UK, and how he has 'contacts' that could help the team get set up with the best horses for the competition."

"Oh please." Katy rolled her eyes. "You can't buy or bribe your way onto the team." Her brow furrowed suddenly and she looked at me. "Can you?"

"*I* don't know," I snapped as everyone's eyes followed hers. "Why're you asking me?"

"Keep your hair on, it was just a question," Katy said, looking offended. "Man, you're sensitive tonight." She leaned back against the kitchen cabinet and nudged the pizza box towards me with her foot. "Eat more pizza. That always cheers AJ up."

AJ ignored her dig. "Speaking of Stacey, I heard she's bought a new horse."

We all looked at AJ with interest. The swapping and changing of horses and ponies was a regular occurrence on the circuit, though it happened mostly at the beginning and end of the season.

"I haven't seen it," Katy said. "She was only riding that fat black thing today."

"Be nice, Gothic's cute," AJ told her.

"There's more to a good pony than how cute it is," Katy retorted.

AJ glared at her. "You only think that because your ponies –"

"Whose horse has Stacey bought?" I asked, interrupting quickly before their bickering got out of hand.

"One of Connor's," Katy said casually. "The one they got from Aussie for Grace." She rolled her eyes disparagingly. "Anna rode it at Nationals, said it's super hot. How Stacey thinks she's doing to ride it when she almost got killed the last time she rode anything hot is beyond me, but you can't fix stupid."

Star. As much as I hated Connor, I still liked that mare. And Katy was right that Stacey wasn't the right rider for her.

"That's going to end badly," I concurred. "I tried that horse last weekend, and it…" It was my turn to be interrupted as my cell phone started ringing. I dug it out of my pocket as AJ and Jonty started arguing over who was going to eat the last piece of pizza, or rather who wasn't, because they were both insisting that the other should have it.

I looked at the screen of my phone to find out who was ringing. *Home.*

"Hello?"

Mum's voice, sounding anxious. "Honey, it's me. There's something wrong with Buck."

I felt as though the ground had fallen out from underneath me. "What? What d'you mean? What's wrong with him?"

Everyone else in the truck had stopped talking and were staring at me in alarm.

"I don't know." I could hear the anxiety in her voice. "I've called the vet, but he's been coughing all day and now he's not breathing properly."

My heart was pounding, and I was having trouble breathing myself. "What'd the vet say?"

"She's on her way now."

I stood up, tossing my half-eaten pizza slice back into the box. I wasn't going to sit around here while Buck needed me. I owed it to him to go home and check on him.

"I'll tell Dad. We'll head out tonight."

Mum didn't argue. "I think that'd be best. I'll ring you back when the vet gets here."

"Okay." She hung up before I could, and I stared at the phone blankly for a moment, then looked around at my friends' concerned faces. "I have to go."

"Is everything okay?"

"I don't know. Buck's sick." I stared down at the warm phone in my hand, wondering how such an innocuous object could be the

bearer of such bad news. "I have to tell Dad. We need to go home."
I was repeating myself, but I couldn't think of anything else to say.

AJ got to her feet next to me. "We'll come and help you pack up."
She put her one good arm around my shoulders and squeezed me
briefly towards her. "He'll be okay."

I wasn't sure about that, and I knew AJ wasn't either. But as we
flowed out of Katy's truck as a group and split up, AJ coming with me
to tell Dad and get the truck ready, the others going to the yards to
collect my ponies and bring them over to load up, I was immensely
grateful that I had friends like these.

8
MAKING PROMISES

Much to Dad's disgust, Lesley was the vet who attended the call-out. Dad had sworn after her last visit that he wouldn't have her back, but you couldn't pick and choose in an emergency.

"Could be a couple of different things," she told us, her calm voice sounding tinny over the truck's speaker phone. It was a three hour drive home from Taihape, and we were still on the road when she called to report her findings. "Hard to say right now. I've given him something to help him breathe, which he's doing a bit more easily now."

Dad's irritation with her was palpable. He liked straight answers, and didn't have much patience for people being unsure what the problem was. "Do you have *any* idea what's affecting him, or are you just taking a stab in the dark?"

Lesley didn't seem perturbed by his anger, maintaining the same calm tone. "It looks like bronchitis. Usually caused by a viral infection, but could be allergic. Has he always been stabled at night?"

"Yes. Ever since we've owned him, and we've had him going on three years now."

"Anything else in his routine changed?"

Dad glanced at me, and I shook my head. "No. Nothing," he told the vet. "Everything's just as it's always been, except that he picked up this cough when we were down at Nationals last week."

"Could be a virus then. Just have to make sure it doesn't get worse, or he could end up with pneumonia. And I've taken blood samples, just in case."

"In case what?" I asked.

"Well, there are a couple of other things that it might be. Just want to be on the safe side, that's all."

"What do you think it might be?" I asked nervously, racking my brains for possibilities.

"Oh, there's a few things." A hesitation came into Lesley's relaxed tone at last, as though there was something she wasn't sure she wanted to say. "He's running a temperature and I don't like the colour of his nasal discharge. He's also got a bit of swelling around his throat. Could just be from all the coughing and breathing trouble he's been having, or…" She hesitated for a moment, then said the words that made my blood run cold. "…it could be a symptom of strangles."

Her voice went fuzzy as we hit a patch of bad reception, and I zoned out while Dad yelled at the phone, as though the volume of his voice would help us get better service. Strangles was rare in New Zealand, but it was present. There'd been a couple of recent cases, and although they'd supposedly been successfully contained, it was highly contagious and spread easily. If Buck had picked it up at Nationals, it would be spreading around the country like wildfire right now. I wrapped my arms around myself, shuddering at the thought of him in the middle of all those ponies in the covered yards. He'd been coughing during the whole show. Skip and Forbes could be infected, and any other pony he came into contact with. My heart pounded at the recollection of Buck touching noses with Grace's pony Summertime at the start of the week. If my pony ended up being responsible for spreading an illness like that right before Horse of the Year, my social outcast status was going to be well and truly fixed for life.

When the line finally cleared, Lesley assured us that it was a highly unlikely scenario, but she thought she'd mention it, just in case.

"It hasn't been around for a while, but we can't rule it out just yet. Keep him isolated from the others," she recommended. "And not stabled, if you can help it. Could just be a dust allergy that's affecting him, so he'd be better off outside. In a small area though, not a big paddock so he's not tempted to run around. He should be able to see your other horses, but not get close to them in case he's infectious. Of course," she added, "it *could* be a pollen allergy, in which case he'd be better off inside. Up to you, really."

I watched Dad's knuckles whiten on the wheel. "Make your bloody mind up! You're supposed to be the expert here. *You* tell us what to do."

Her steady voice remained calm. "Well like I said, it depends on what's causing it. But if he was mine, I'd put him outside. Rug him up so he's warm but not overheating, and keep him in a small, sheltered paddock with a medium amount of grass. Take him off hay and chaff for a few days to see if that makes a difference. If you must feed him hay, make sure you soak it. Sorry, but I've got to go. I've got a colic to treat. Ring me in the morning and let me know how he's getting on."

And the line went dead.

Dad was livid, raging the whole way home about useless vets who couldn't make a decision to save their lives, and how they wouldn't give anyone a straight answer any more in case they were wrong and got sued for it. I didn't point out that he would be the first person to sue if someone misdiagnosed Buck. I knew that Lesley was right that there were any number of things that could be wrong with Buck. I only hoped that we weren't looking at the worst case scenario.

Dad straightened up and wiped his forehead with the back of his arm. "Think that'll do it?"

I nodded, lowering the torch and looking around. We hadn't had rain in weeks, and the grass was dry and burnt across our whole property. Finding somewhere to paddock Buck that wasn't too dusty had been the only thing I'd been able to get Dad to discuss reasonably on the way home. In the end, we'd settled for the back lawn, which had been watered by Mum's sprinkler system all summer and was the only green grass we had. We'd had to put up electrical tape around the borders to keep Buck off the flowerbeds – not because Dad or I cared particularly about Mum's plants, but because we were worried that he'd eat something he shouldn't and make himself even sicker.

Not that he looked very interested in eating anything. I haltered him in the barn and led him out to the lawn, and he walked slowly behind me with his head down. I told myself that it was just the sedation that Lesley had given him taking a while to wear off, and that he'd be perkier in the morning. I led him through the tape gate that Dad was holding open, and stopped him in the middle of the lawn. Buck looked around with vague interest for a second, then sighed and lowered his head again.

I unbuckled his halter and slipped it off, then slid a hand under his cover to test his body temperature. He felt warm, and I was worried about him overheating. But if he had pneumonia, I didn't want him to get a chill, and he was still running a temperature. I wished I knew what to do. I leaned my head against his neck and closed my eyes, listening to the rustling of the trees that surrounded the lawn. At least I'd be able to look out of my bedroom window and check on him.

Skip whinnied from the paddock, where he'd been turned out with Forbes. I'd put them out before I'd been allowed anywhere near Buck, in case he was infectious. They'd both had run around in the paddock like idiots once I'd let them go. Buck had barely reacted at the time, which had worried me, but as Skip's high-pitched whinny rang out in the night air, Buck lifted his head and let out a throaty attempt at a whinny himself.

I wrapped my arms around his proud neck and hugged him gently. "Feel better soon. I'll be down to check on you as soon as it's light."

Buck lowered his head again, and I let him go. He sniffed at the grass at his feet, then sighed, disinterested in food, and I walked back to the gate where Dad was waiting. I hated leaving my pony when he wasn't well. It felt wrong.

"I think I'll sleep out here tonight," I told my father.

I expected him to argue, but he just shrugged. "If you like."

I nodded, looking back over my shoulder at the dark silhouette of my pony. I couldn't let anything happen to him. Not on my watch.

I owed him that.

I woke at dawn, as the birds in the garden started announcing the morning. Stirring slowly, the world came to me in a grey haze at first, and it took me a moment to realise where I was, and to remember why. Then it came back to me, and I sat up quickly, looking around for Buck. For a few heart-stopping seconds, I couldn't see him at all, but then I located his dark shape standing under the kowhai tree. Struggling out of my sleeping bag, I walked barefoot across the cold grass and spoke softly to him.

Buck turned his head and looked at me, his ears swivelling forward. His eyes were a little brighter, but he still looked miserable. Any dreams I'd had of a miracle recovery were scuppered by the sight of him, and I slipped a hand under his thick rug again to check his temperature. His coat felt damp, and I unbuckled the cover and pulled it back to reveal that he was sweating. Guiltily, I stripped the rug off and ran to the tack room for a lighter one. It only took me a few minutes to find his one, but by the time I got back to Buck's side he was shivering slightly in the cool morning breeze.

"Sorry buddy."

I threw the lighter cover over him and fastened it quickly, trying not to think about the way his belly was tucked up under his ribs. Whatever the vet had given him yesterday hadn't worked. I was supposed to ring Lesley this morning and give her an update, but knowing Dad, he'd refuse to have her back and be looking for another opinion. I bundled up the discarded cover into my arms and took it to the gate, then stopped. If Buck had strangles, this rug would be contagious. And I'd touched him, then gone into the stables and touched all the covers on the racks. I dropped the rug onto the wet grass and sank down on top of it, furious with myself. Balling my hands into fists, I thumped the heavy cover angrily. My temper flared, raged inside me like an angry beast, and I let it take over, punching and kicking the cover until I was out of breath. I threw it as far from me as I could and stood there staring at it, sweat breaking out on my skin despite the morning chill. Buck was staring at me in alarm, his nostrils flared wide.

I took a step towards him and he widened his eyes and snorted nervously. I stopped, then went back to my sleeping bag and crawled back into it, screwing my eyes shut and trying to fall back asleep. Maybe when I woke up, this would all turn out to be a bad dream.

When I did finally get up, I retrieved Buck's discarded cover as well as my sleeping bag and carried everything onto the back porch. I dumped it by the door and went into the kitchen, my stomach rumbling as I left a trail of damp grass-flecked footprints across the cold tiles.

Mum was up already, sipping coffee and flicking through emails on her laptop as she stood at the kitchen counter.

"Morning."

Her eyes scanned my appearance with displeasure. "Have you been sleeping in the barn?"

"No. On the back lawn." I pulled an almost-empty box of muesli out of the pantry and put it on the table. "Buck's not any better, by the way. Thanks for asking."

Mum shot me a look, but didn't say anything. She set her coffee down on the bench and started typing rapidly, staring at the laptop screen with rapt attention. I made my breakfast and sat down to eat it, wondering whether I should ring Lesley and see what she thought, or just wait for Dad to call someone else out.

Mum's typing paused, and I thought of something I'd been meaning to ask her.

"Why did you ring me last night?"

"What?" Mum looked confused. "Because I thought you'd want to know."

"I did, but that's not what I meant." I stirred the muesli in my bowl, fishing for words. "Why didn't you ring Dad?"

Mum pursed her lips. "He's your pony, isn't he?"

No, not technically, I wanted to say. *He belongs to you and Dad.* But I knew that wasn't what she wanted to hear, so I just shrugged.

"Would you rather I hadn't?" Mum sounded annoyed now, and I tried to placate her.

"No. I'm glad you rang me. I just thought it was weird, that's all."

The weirdest part was that it hadn't actually occurred to me that it was strange until I'd burst into our truck last night and told Dad the news. He'd just stared at me for a moment, then looked down at his own phone, as though checking for a missed call. He hadn't hesitated for long, understanding the urgency of the situation, and he'd got straight on the phone with Mum while we packed up the truck, but I could tell it was bothering him the whole way home from Taihape.

"I thought I had a better chance of reaching you," Mum said. "I know what you're like with that phone, it's never out of your hand."

I pretended to accept that lame excuse. I pretended that it wasn't about her and Dad, about the fact that they barely talked to each other anymore, about the way she'd thrown herself so much into her work lately that she hardly seemed to notice me. For years, I'd been the centre of her universe. I hadn't always appreciated that, and part of me was grateful for the breathing space she'd been giving me lately, but this recent disinterest was something else entirely, and I didn't know what to make of it.

I ate another mouthful of muesli, resisting the urge to ask her how often she'd checked on Buck yesterday, and how long he'd been distressed for. I wasn't sure I wanted answers to those questions.

Mum set down her coffee cup on the bench with a thunk. "I'm heading out. I've got clients to visit all day."

"Okay." I picked up the muesli box on the kitchen table and rattled the dregs at her. "There's not much left. Can you get some more?"

"I'm not your slave," she snapped. I stared at her, taken aback, and her face softened. "I don't have time, darling. But I think supermarkets deliver these days, don't they? Why don't you see if you can set that up for us? Order whatever we need. Put it on your father's credit card." She picked up her handbag and slung it over her shoulder. The expensive Italian leather bumped against her hip as she gathered her laptop bag and a huge book of fabric samples. "Have a nice day. I'll see you later."

I looked at the puddle of greyish milk that lay at the bottom of my bowl, listening to my mother leave the house. I should be happy for her that she was finally taking charge of her own life, and not letting Dad push her around anymore. I'd resented her for that, so why was I mad at her for doing the opposite?

I didn't have the answers to those questions. I didn't have any answers right now, but it was time to track down someone who might.

"He's not looking much better, is he?"

Lesley was observing Buck critically as I held him on the back lawn. His sides were tucked up and his breathing was still laboured.

"No." I was direct with her. The sun beat down on our heads as she opened her veterinary kit and pulled out a bright pink stethoscope. I was glad Dad wasn't here to see it. I didn't think he'd be impressed.

"So how is the old man?"

I blinked, confused. "My dad?"

Lesley raised her eyebrows. "I meant the pony."

"Oh." I felt my face flush, and I spoke quickly to try and avoid further embarrassment. "Lethargic. Not as interested in food as he is usually, although he ate his bran mash this morning."

"Pooping normally?"

I nodded. "Not as much as usual, but yeah, otherwise."

"Has he been drinking?" She slipped the stethoscope buds into her ears, then turned back to me with a grin. "And I'm still asking about the pony."

I couldn't help a slight smile at that one. "Yes, a little." I'd topped his water bucket up that morning, but he hadn't exactly drained it overnight.

"Okay." She nudged Buck's left foreleg forward a little, then positioned the end of the stethoscope just behind his elbow. I stood quietly, waiting, as she listened while counting off the seconds on her wristwatch. I watched Buck's sides heave in and out as he breathed, occasionally swatting flies listlessly with his tail.

"Forty-eight beats per minute," she said, removing the stethoscope from her ears and stepping back from my pony.

"That's high," I replied with a frown. "And his respiration rate is twenty four, which is high too."

Lesley looked surprised. "Were you counting?"

I nodded. "I was watching his sides move, and counted while you did. Fifteen seconds, right? Then multiply by four."

"Correct." She seemed impressed, but I was too worried about Buck to care. "Don't panic too much, okay? It's not ideal, but we expected the heart and respiration to be up, considering his condition. And I've seen worse."

I wasn't sure that was too comforting, but I nodded. She placed the stethoscope higher, listening carefully to his lungs for a few seconds at a time.

"Bit of wheezing going on, but that's expected too, given what we can see from the outside." She laid a hand over Buck's side, watching the expansion and contraction of his ribcage. "I'll give him an injection to try and settle things down. Looks like a respiratory infection, which is treatable, although it might limit his future endeavours."

"I don't care about that," I told her. "I just want him to feel better."

"Good to know." Lesley moved to Buck's hind end and prepared to take his temperature again. "He's a show jumper, isn't he?"

I nodded. "One of the best."

She smiled. "He's certainly very well looked after." She inserted the thermometer and looked around the garden, one arm resting casually on Buck's rump. "Nice place you've got here. What are those, petunias?"

I followed her gaze instinctively, then shrugged. "I don't know."

"I think they are. My mother's mad keen on gardening," Lesley confessed. "Every time I go round there she's dragging me out to admire her garden. Not much a gardener myself, I'm afraid. Too busy to have time to look after it. Only thing I can grow is weeds." The thermometer beeped, and she pulled it out and looked at it. "Thirty nine point two. Gone down a bit from yesterday then."

"That's still high."

"It is."

"But you've seen worse, right?"

Lesley smiled at me. "That I have. Now, what've I got in here to make you feel better, eh old man?"

She rummaged around in her kit while I stroked Buck's face gently. He lowered his head to lean against me, and half-closed his eyes. I could feel the effort of his breathing as it reverberated through his whole body, and I fought back tears. I just wanted him to be okay again. I ran my hand across his cheek and over his throat, which was still swollen.

"You said yesterday that it might be st...strangles," I said, choking on the word.

Lesley looked up from her kit, sympathy in her eyes. "I said worst case scenario, and he's not presenting many symptoms of it. That swelling around his throat could just be grass glands, so let's not jump to any conclusions. I'll get the swab test results back in a few days. In the meantime," she continued, standing up and drawing a clear liquid into a small syringe as she spoke, "we'll give him something to make him feel better."

Lesley pulled out a flap of Buck's skin, then slid the needle into his neck. Buck hardly flinched as she slowly depressed the plunger until all of the liquid had disappeared, then carefully withdrew the needle.

"Keep a close eye on him for the rest of the day, and ring me if anything changes," she said. "If this doesn't help, there are a few other things we can try. Some of them get a bit pricey though."

"That's not an issue for us," I assured her, and she nodded.

"Didn't think it would be," she replied as she packed up her kit. "You've got my number, haven't you? Stay in touch." She straightened up and gave Buck a gentle pat on the neck. "Feel better, old boy."

Buck shook his head and turned to look at her, as though he was saying thank you for helping him.

"How long until the drugs take effect?" I asked.

"You should see an improvement within a couple of hours, but it might not last," Lesley warned me. "So keep a close eye on him. Are you back at school tomorrow?"

I pulled a face, and nodded.

"You have my sympathies," she said with a slight smile. "Well, as long as there's someone around during the day to keep an eye on him."

"Dad's planning on working from home tomorrow. That's why he's at the office today," I told her, and she nodded approval.

"Good for him. Try not to panic, okay? Whatever it is, it's unlikely to kill him."

She scooped up her kit and walked off across the lawn. I wished her words made me feel better.

"Susannah?"

"Here," I mumbled reflexively.

Voices giggled around me, and I looked up at Miss Rutherford, who was scowling at me from behind her desk.

"I've already called the roll," she reminded me. "I'm calling you now about this."

She raised her hand, waving a yellow slip of paper in my direction. My classmates started whispering, and a few heads turned to look at me as I stood up, cursing whoever's idea it had been to colour-code those slips. Blue slips came from the office, pink slips from the Dean, and yellow slips from the guidance counsellor. I still hadn't responded to Ms Bryant's more subtle requests for a meeting with me this term, but it didn't look like she'd given up on me. Just on subtlety.

I plucked the yellow slip out of Miss Rutherford's talons and scrunched it in my hand as I walked back to my desk, the hot flush in my cheeks betraying my embarrassment to the rest of the room.

Callie shot me a sympathetic look as I sat back down and shoved the balled-up slip into my bag.

"Can't she take a hint?" I muttered. "If I wanted to talk to her, I'd have done it already."

"You should go to the guidance office and complain about being harassed. By *her*," Callie told me.

"I actually should. Or I could just keep ignoring her."

"That's a better plan. It's not like there aren't enough screwed-up people in this school to keep her busy. Why does she want to talk to the normal ones?"

I shrugged, pleased that Callie considered me to be normal. I wasn't sure that *I* did, but I wasn't about to disagree with her.

"So how'd your party go?" I asked her. "Sorry I missed it."

"You didn't," she told me. "I had to postpone. My great-grandma had a stroke on Friday night, and my parents thought it was inappropriate to hold a party."

"Oh my gosh, that's awful! Is she okay?"

Callie nodded. "Yeah. Well, as good as she can be. She's had a few strokes now, and every time the doctors say that the next one will be the last, but she keeps battling on." She frowned, her perfect eyebrows flexing inwards. "Sometimes I think she'd be better off if she didn't. I know that sounds callous, but she can't even eat on her own any more. I wouldn't want that kind of life."

"Me either. That's terrible though, I'm sorry."

"The doctors were the worst," Callie said bitterly. "They had my parents really wound up, saying that it was touch and go and to say our final goodbyes. And the next morning she was breathing on her own and had perked right up. But enough of that, it's too depressing to talk about. The good news is that I get to have my party this weekend instead. So you'll be able to come!"

"I…"

"You're not going horse showing *again*, are you?" Callie asked, seeming astonished that I would consider competing two weeks in a row.

"Well, no," I admitted. Even if Buck hadn't been sick, we'd planned to have the weekend off, although what was supposed to be a quiet weekend to prepare for Horse of the Year had turned into an enforced segregation. Until the strangles test came back negative, we couldn't take any of the ponies off the property. And if it didn't come back negative…well, I didn't even want to think about that possibility.

"Perfect!" Callie beamed. "So you'll come to my party."

"I don't know," I said. "One of my ponies is really sick, and I don't like leaving him."

Callie looked surprised. "But you leave him to go to school," she pointed out.

"Only because I have to."

"I'm sure he'll be better by then," she said confidently. "He's not dying, is he?"

I pushed down the fear that bubbled inside me at the thought. "No. I don't think so."

"He'll be fine," she assured me. "And you *have* to come to the party. It's going to be amazing. I think it was actually a good thing that I've had to delay it, I mean, not because of what happened to my Grammy because obviously that was terrible but now I've got more time to plan and invite people. And there's a couple of guys that you *have* to meet. I actually can't wait to introduce you. Now, what're you going to wear?"

9

WORTH FIGHTING FOR

I knocked on the open door of the guidance office, and Ms Bryant looked up. "There you are, Susannah. Come on in, and shut the door behind you."

The small room was stiflingly warm. A slight breeze coming through the window provided little relief as I dropped my bag at my feet and sat down in the chair.

"I'm glad you've managed to come and see me," Miss Bryant smiled, sounding genuine. "I've been wanting to catch up with you since the beginning of term."

I crossed one leg over the other and said nothing. She knew as well as I did that I was only here because I'd received my third summons in as many days, and had finally caved in to her demands just to get her off my back. I'd been to see her last year, had talked through some things and ended up telling her far more than I'd ever intended to about my family situation. At the time, it had seemed helpful, but now I found the fact that she knew so much about me unnerving, and I wasn't in a hurry to divulge any new information.

"So how are things going so far this year? Are you getting along okay in your classes?"

I nodded. "Yeah, fine."

"No problems with your teachers, or other students?" she pressed, watching closely as I shook my head. "Coursework all making sense so far?"

"Yep." I folded my arms across my chest, then unfolded them again. I didn't want to appear defensive, even though I knew that was already how I sounded.

Ms Bryant leaned back in her chair and continued smiling at me. "That's great to hear. And how are those lovely ponies of yours? Did you have a successful summer?"

Smart woman. She knew that talking about my ponies was one way to break the ice – it's how she'd got me talking before. I hesitated, but couldn't resist.

"It was okay. Skip's good. Forbes has his good days and his bad ones." I paused, then pushed on. "Buck's not so good. He picked up a cold at Nationals and seems to have developed a respiratory infection." I still couldn't say the word *strangles*.

"Oh no! That doesn't sound good," Ms Bryant said. She sounded genuinely concerned, much more interested than Callie had been. But then, it was her job to pretend to be interested in other people's problems.

I shrugged, trying to bite my tongue, but I needed to talk about this. So much for playing things close to the chest. "We've had the vet out a couple of times, but she's still not quite sure what's going on. He gets better with medication, but then he goes downhill again once it's worn off. We don't know what's causing it, and it's just really hard to watch him struggling to breathe."

The stuffy room felt oppressive, the air pooling thickly around me. I could feel my own lungs straining slightly, and wondered if this was how Buck felt. Ms Bryant continued to make sympathetic noises about my pony's predicament, while I felt sweat beginning to bead on the back of my neck and under my arms.

"Don't you have air conditioning?" I asked.

Ms Bryant smiled, as though she was used to the question. "I do, but unfortunately it's broken. There's a fan over there that you can switch on, if you like."

I looked over at the wobbly fan, standing forlornly in the corner of the small room. Ms Bryant didn't seem bothered by the lack of airflow, despite her flushed skin and short-sleeved shirt, so I let it be. She took a sip of water from a glass on her desk and smiled at me.

"So what's good with you right now?"

"Huh?"

"What's going well in your life? What are you working towards, what goals do you have for the year?"

"Um. You mean academically?"

"If you like, but I meant in general." She opened her arms, spread them wide. "Anything. You have a leave application in for the Horse of the Year Show, which is coming up soon. You must be looking forward to that."

I nodded. "Yeah, I guess." I didn't want to talk about my chances in Pony of the Year. I racked my brains for something to deflect her with, and landed on Ireland. "There's an international team competition coming up that I've applied for," I told Ms Bryant, trying to put the excitement into my voice that I couldn't muster for Pony of the Year. "I think I've got a decent chance at being selected."

"Ooh, how exciting!" Nobody could ever accuse Ms Bryant of lacking enthusiasm. "When is it, and where will it be held?"

"Ireland, in June. It's a show jumping team event, and they're taking six riders from New Zealand to compete in three shows against the British and Irish home teams. And possibly some Europeans at the last one, I don't really know."

As I spoke, I found myself starting to get excited about it. I really wanted to be on the team. Not only for the travel opportunities – I'd never been to Ireland – but being selected for a team would make me feel as though I was part of the show jumping scene in a way I never had been before.

"Sounds wonderful! When do you find out if you've been picked?"

I shrugged. "Soon, I guess. The team will be announced before the end of the month. Then they're running training camps every month through to the competition, so it's pretty intense but it's a great opportunity."

I'd spent a couple of hours on Facebook last night, chatting with Katy as we'd both read up on the competition's rules and format. Details were still light, but the prospect was thrilling. As Katy messaged me into the night with any number of plans and predictions, it was hard to remember that we hadn't been friends at all only a few months ago. In her mind, we were as good as selected. But I wasn't willing to get my hopes up too far. There was still a chance, as outside as it seemed, that someone else would beat one – or even both – of us into the squad.

"Brilliant. Well, good luck!" Ms Bryant said, threading her fingers together and resting her chin on her knuckles. "Is there anything that the school can do to help you get there? Any fundraising, or publicity?"

I winced at the thought, although I appreciated the sentiment. "Um, I don't think so. And I haven't been picked yet, so…"

"Of course." She glanced at her watch, and frowned. "You'll keep me in the loop though, won't you?"

"Okay."

"Promise?"

"Yeah."

"Good. Now. There's another reason that I wanted to talk to you today."

I shifted uneasily in my seat, waiting for a barrage of questions that I didn't want to answer, but she surprised me by opening a file on her desk and pulling out a piece of paper, then handing it to me.

"Do you recognise this?"

I scanned the page, then looked back at her with a frown. "Yes."

"Mrs Kilbourne passed it along to me at the end of last week," she explained.

"I got Merit for this," I pointed out, looking back down at the poem I'd written for English. I'd left it until the very last minute, when I'd found myself sitting in front of my laptop with only a few minutes to midnight, desperately trying to think of something to say. I'd spent the evening trawling through Facebook, looking at photos from Nationals, trying not to notice the comments that people had posted. But when I'd come to one of Anna riding Star, my traitorous eye hadn't been able to avoid seeing my name. And once I'd seen it, I'd had to read it.

Anna and Stacey had engaged in a spirited discussion about Star's merits, which they rated highly, and Stacey's recent purchase of the mare, which they considered to be a relief in the face of the possibility that she had almost been sold to me. Anna, in particular, continued to profess her horror at the thought, as though Stacey, who tended to drop her horses at the base of the jump and operate on a 'when in doubt, speed up' policy, was going to do better than I could have. But it was Connor's comment that had stung the most. He'd only written one, but it was enough.

Haha I knew the fastest way to sell Star would be to make the rest of the world feel sorry for her and want to save her from that fate!! Never wouldve gone thru with it don't worry

I'd clicked away then, but I hadn't been able to erase the words from my mind. For the next two hours, as I lay in bed trying to fall asleep, I was plagued by memories of the things I'd said and done in the past to make them all hate me so much. And finally, as the clock ticked towards midnight, I'd sat up, flipped my laptop open, and written my poetry assignment.

Sometimes I step outside myself and watch the things I do
I judge her from afar, that girl, and know that you do too.
I want to tell her 'stand up straight' and 'wipe away that frown'
I want her to be welcomed in and never be let down.

I know inside she's hurting and she just wants to belong
I know deep down she's smiling but her face just shows it wrong.
I know what you all think of her and the prejudice you hold
I know you want to make her pay for things you have been told.
But trust me when I tell you that the guilt is always there
The pain, regret, the scars inside and most of all the fear.
She is most afraid, that girl, that you might look inside
You'll see past her exterior and what it is you'll find.
She wants to be deemed worthy, to be held up to the light
She wants her trespasses absolved but cannot make things right.
Because deep down inside herself, she doesn't know for sure
If she is any good at all
If she's worth fighting for.

I felt my face flush hot as I re-read those embarrassingly emotional words. But surely the rest of the class wrote poetry like that too – didn't they? Were teenage girls actually capable of writing poetry that *wasn't* emotional and depressing? Maybe the rest of the class had been smart, and written a witty limerick, or taken Callie's advice and just scrawled out a few random words and left it to Mrs Kilbourne to make sense of it.

Too late now. I handed the poem back to Ms Bryant, who returned it to the folder on her desk. I wished I'd ripped it up instead.

"I'm sorry that you feel that way, Susannah."

"It's just a poem."

"Is it?" The bell rang, and I stood up quickly, overcome with relief. Ms Bryant's smile was slightly rueful. "Always so eager to leave."

I shrugged as I picked up my bag. I couldn't wait to get out of this stifling room. "Well, I've got Bio now, and it's all the way over the other side of school, so..."

"Of course. Well I'm going to leave it up to you whether you come back and talk to me again. You know that my door's always open."

Sure it was. "Thanks." I opened the door and felt a rush of cooler air brush against my overheated skin. Relief. "Maybe when the weather's cooler and it's not so stuffy in here," I told Ms Bryant, trying to deflect her with a joke.

But this time, she didn't smile. "You could've turned the fan on." She fixed me with a serious look that I couldn't quite read. "You don't have to sit there and take it when things in life make you uncomfortable, Susannah. You just have to make a decision, then follow through with it." She picked up the folder containing my poem and slid it into the filing cabinet behind her desk. "Don't be afraid to go after the things you want."

Ms Bryant pushed the filing drawer shut, then leaned over and switched on the fan. It whirred into life, and she smiled as she let it blow air across her, cooling her skin. I realised then that she hadn't been any more comfortable with the sweltering heat than I had been. So why sit there and do nothing? She could've stood up and turned the fan on herself.

So could you. I couldn't help feeling as though I'd just failed a test I hadn't realised I'd been taking. Ms Bryant closed her eyes as she stood in front of the fan, and I stepped out into the hall, leaving the door open behind me.

"Will there be boys there?"

"It's not being held in a convent," I told my father at dinner that night. He narrowed his eyes at me as I stabbed my fork into the green beans on my plate. "Yes. There will be boys at the party. But Callie's parents will be there too, and it'll be well-supervised." I had no idea whether that was true, but it sounded good.

"What about alcohol?"

"It's a *party*, Dad."

"It's a party that you're not going to, then. Don't forget that you're underage."

I was tempted, for a moment, to ask him where his concern had been when he'd let me go off unsupervised to Connor's truck at Nationals, but I bit my tongue. He didn't need to know any of that.

"What if I promise not to drink?" I offered. I didn't want to anyway. I hadn't liked the way it had made me feel, fuzzy and slow to react. I wanted my wits about me if I was going to Callie's party. I wasn't sure that I really wanted to. A small part of me relished my father's refusal, and I rehearsed breaking the news to Callie inside my head. *My dad won't let me go. He's stuck in the dark ages.* I imagined her irritation, and sympathy.

"Of course you can go to the party, darling," Mum said, sipping her wine and smiling at me.

Dad glowered down the table at her. "I just said she couldn't."

"Well maybe it's not up to you." Mum looked at me. "Do you want to go?"

"Yes," I lied, though I wasn't sure why.

"Then you can go," Mum said determinedly, slicing calmly into her salmon fillet and ignoring my father.

"Since when do you get to overrule me?" he asked, his voice dangerously quiet.

"Since when do you get to make all of the decisions?" Mum snapped back, startling us both. "Susie's almost sixteen, and if she wants to go to a well-supervised party at a friend's house, I'm not going to stop her. You let Pete go to parties when he was her age."

Dad's expression froze at the mention of his estranged son. I could see him battling between continuing to refuse to acknowledge that Pete even existed and the desire to rebut my mother's comment. His predilection for arguing overruled, just as I'd known it would.

"Well, it's different for boys."

Mum rolled her eyes. "Maybe in *your* day."

"Are you arguing with the statistics?" Dad challenged her. "Because I read –"

I stood up, my chair scraping on the tiles. "May I be excused?"

Their heads swivelled in my direction. Dad spoke first. "No. We're discussing your request to attend this party, so if you want a verdict you'd better sit back down and listen."

"It's not much of a discussion if I don't even get a say," I pointed out. "And you're not discussing, you're arguing. Again." The last word killed me to say aloud, but it was true. If my parents weren't avoiding each other lately, they were bickering, sniping at one another constantly. I didn't know where it was going to lead, but my money was on 'nowhere good'.

"Fine. Let's hear your side. Why should I let you go to this party?"

"Why shouldn't you?" I countered. "I already told you that I won't drink. You can breathalyse me at the end of the night if you want to, I don't care. But this is kind of a big deal for me." I rested my hands on the edge of the table and stared at the new glass salt and pepper grinders sitting in the centre. "I'm finally making friends at school – proper friends who want to see me outside of school. Do you realise how long it's been since I last had that? And Callie asked me to come to this party, and she was actually disappointed last weekend when I couldn't, because it clashed with Taihape. So now she's really excited that I can go because I'm not showing this weekend, and if I don't go, she'll think I don't like her and I'll be friendless again." I winced internally at how pitiful I sounded.

"You're not friendless."

"Aren't I? How often do I have friends over after school? How many of my friends can you actually name?"

"You've got the ponies to ride after school, you don't have time to have people over," Dad argued. "And I can name three. AJ, Katy, and…er…"

I rolled my eyes so hard that it actually hurt, but I couldn't help myself. "Thanks for making my point. Besides, they're horse show friends. And they're great, but they don't go to my school. I'm lonely,

Dad. I like having friends. I want to have more friends. Please don't keep making this so hard for me."

He said nothing, just stared at his plate for a moment, then looked across at my mother. She seemed torn between expressing pity towards me and shooting smug looks at my father. As though she hadn't been as bad as him for most of my life. Keeping me on lockdown after school and at shows, vetting all of my friends to make sure that their parents were socially acceptable in her own limited circle, organising playdates with her friends' kids while quietly manoeuvring anyone she considered undesirable out of my life. Why had it taken me so long to realise that, and so much longer to take a stand against it?

"Fine." Dad set his knife and fork down on his plate and stood up, abandoning the remnants of his meal. "I give up. You can go. But no drinking. And no smoking."

I nodded. "Does marijuana count?"

The slightest flicker of amusement crossed his face, but he reined it in. "What do you think?"

"I'll be good," I told him. "I promise."

I checked the time and clicked Refresh, feeling my palms sweat as I watched the computer screen reload. The team for Ireland was supposed to be announced at 5pm, but it was ten past five and still no word. I scrolled down my Facebook feed again, searching for any alerts from ESNZ. In this world of social media, they'd decided to announce the team on Facebook. It seemed strangely unprofessional to me, but as neither Katy nor I (nor anyone else she had talked to) had heard anything from the selectors since the confirmation email that our applications had been received, it seemed that they'd decided to do away with social niceties in favour of social media.

Still nothing. I hit Refresh again, and then suddenly there it was. The ESNZ logo on the left, and the text underneath that was about to tell me whether I was going to Ireland – or staying home.

We are thrilled to announce the New Zealand Young Rider team who will be travelling to Ireland in June to represent our country. The team will be: Senior (U21) Imogen Davis-Blake & Ellie Warren, Intermediate (U18) Charlotte Yeats & Anna Harcourt; Junior (U16) Katy O'Reilly... *Continue reading.*

I clicked those last words, pleased for Katy's success as my own hopes soared. The text took a moment to load, and I crossed my fingers and toes even tighter until the rest of the message appeared.

...& Lily Christianson. Chef d'equipe will be Maureen Yeats, and Dennis Foxhall-James will coach. Congratulations to our successful riders. Non-travelling reserves will be named shortly.

There was more, but I stopped reading. Sat still and stared at the words on the screen for a moment, then closed my eyes, letting the disappointment sink in.

I heard my father's footsteps cross the landing from his bedroom, and he stopped in the doorway of my room. "Any word yet?"

I took a breath before I opened my eyes and at him, dreading his reaction. "Yeah, they announced it."

He was frowning, sensing the bad news. "And?"

"They picked Katy," I said, doing my best to sound pleased for my friend. "And Lily." The bitterness that I was trying not to feel slipped off my tongue, betraying my emotions.

Dad was, predictably, livid. "WHAT?!"

I stood up, unable to face the barrage of criticism that he was about to unleash. He wouldn't start out by blaming me. At first it would be the selectors at fault, then the coaches of the team, then Lily's parents, who would've probably bribed the selectors in the first place. But soon enough, the focus would shift, and it would become what I could've done better. Where I'd gone wrong. And I couldn't face it. My own disappointment was bad enough, without having to deal with his as well.

I pushed my way past him and ran down the stairs towards the front door, my thoughts whirling. What was it that Katy had said, sitting in her truck at Taihape? *If they put that kid in the team, then I'd pull out. I'm not even kidding.*

But she had been kidding. No way was she going to reject the opportunity of a lifetime in protest of the team's selection. I didn't expect her to, and I wouldn't want her to. This was my loss, not hers. I grabbed the handle of the front door, pulled it open and almost collided with Mum, her hands full of wallpaper samples.

"Careful!" she told me, but uncharacteristically for her, she didn't seem mad. "Give me a hand to bring this stuff in, would you?"

"I can't." I kept my eyes down as I pulled my boots on. "I've got to ride."

She made an annoyed tutting noise and stepped past me, then stopped in the doorway. "Did you hear about the team yet?"

I zipped up the leather boot and forced myself to stand up straight. "I didn't get in."

"Oh, that's a shame. I'm sorry."

But she didn't sound sorry. I'd expected her to, had expected her to be as disappointed as I was, to drop everything onto the gleaming hallway floor and give me a sympathetic hug. I'd braced myself, knowing that I could hold back the tears that were prickling the corners of my eyes in the face of Dad's raging, but that they would spill in seconds if Mum offered me some kind of sympathy. If she'd said or done anything that wasn't yelling or blame.

But she just seemed ambivalent, and I suddenly wondered how she'd have reacted if I *had* made it into the team. Would she have whooped, and punched the air, and hugged me tight? Or would she have given me the same lacklustre response that I was getting right now?

"Yeah. Oh well."

And I went outside, leaving the front door wide open behind me.

Half an hour later, Dad found me in the stables, saddling Skip.

"I've called Bruce, but I had to leave a message." I looked at him, wishing I was confused by what he meant. But I knew exactly where this was going, and sure enough, moments later he confirmed it. "This makes no sense. Why would they choose that girl instead of you? It's politics, that's what it is. Dirty politics, and probably money changing hands. Well, I won't stand for it. We're not taking this lying down. I'm going to petition them to –"

"Don't." I buckled Skip's girth as he tore at the haynet I'd given him to keep him quiet. "Just leave it, okay? It doesn't matter."

"Of course it matters! How can you say it doesn't matter?"

Skip stopped chewing and looked at us anxiously, so I turned and walked towards the tack room with Dad on my heels. My pony didn't need to be yelled at any more than I did, but at least I could get him out of the firing line. He hadn't done anything wrong, and neither had I. We weren't the ones to blame. It was about time that Dad realised that.

"This is your fault, you know."

Dad stared at me, his mouth half-open in shock. "Excuse me?"

"They were never going to pick me, but not because of me, and not because I can't ride. Because of you." He crossed his arms over his chest, but I pushed on. "You'd ruined my chances before we even got the forms in when you picked that stupid argument with Lily and her dad at Nationals."

Dad sputtered, affecting disbelief. "What, that debacle at the practice fence? That was nothing!"

"Wrong. It was everything. Lily was in the right that day, and you weren't. But nobody wanted to fight with you, because they knew you wouldn't back down, even when you were wrong. You thought you won, but you didn't. You lost that day." I picked up Skip's bridle and untwisted the reins. "You lost for us both."

"You're being ridiculous," he snapped, still in denial.

"No, I'm being honest," I replied. I stared at the faded rosettes on the wall behind him, unable to look at the anger on his face while I said what I'd been waiting for years to say. "Someone told me recently that I don't have to sit there and take life as it comes. That I can stand up and go after what I want. So here's what I want. I want you to back off and stop trying to bully everyone, because you're no better than anyone else and I'm not going to be dragged down with you." I pulled my eyes to meet his. "Not anymore."

"That is *enough*," Dad said, his voice deepening to a growl. "You need to watch your mouth."

"Why? What are you going to do, disown me too?"

I hadn't meant to say that, hadn't even known the words would be there. They'd just slipped out, but the furious look on Dad's face confirmed my fears. For a moment, I wondered if he might really do it. If he would be able to wake up in the morning and know that he'd thrown both of his children out of his life. If he would be able to live with that. I didn't know the answer, but I knew one thing for sure – that the very thought of it terrified me. My father and I didn't always see eye to eye, but the threat of abandonment was suddenly very real. I felt myself start to shake, felt the tears gathering in the corners of my eyes, threatening to spill.

"I would *never* do that," Dad said, his voice quieter than I'd expected it to be.

I looked at him again as I wiped my eyes and saw the sorrow in his eyes. I wanted so badly to believe him.

"Wouldn't you?" I asked. "Why not? You did it once already."

He clenched his teeth together, and sucked in a breath around them, visibly holding his temper by a thread. "What do you want from me?"

So many things. I went with the one that was currently at the front of my mind. "I want you to let Pete come home."

Dad scoffed. "You think that'd improve public opinion?"

"I don't care. I don't care what other people say."

"And if he doesn't want to come back?"

I leaned against the saddle rack on the wall, feeling the metal dig into my back. My voice trembled as I spoke. "You could ask."

Dad looked away from me, arms tightly crossed over his chest as he looked out into the aisle. "I think he's made up his mind."

You mean you have. I gave up. "Fine. Ignore him, abandon him, pretend he never existed. But in case you haven't noticed, you're on the verge of losing Mum too."

Words I never thought I'd say out loud were just tumbling out of me, and Dad's eyes snapped back to mine. I'd expected shock, outrage, anger in his eyes. But I saw something completely different.

Defeat.

It was as though he already knew. He knew that she was going to leave him. She'd talked about it a few months ago, moving us back to South Africa and leaving Dad here. I'd dug my heels in, and Dad had apologised, and things had gone back to normal for a while. But the resurrection of her interior design career hadn't been a spurious decision. She'd found her independence at last. I would've been happier for her if I wasn't so sure it involved leaving us behind.

Because I already knew that if Mum really did leave, if she really did go back to South Africa, she would be going alone. I couldn't leave. I belonged here, and I was staying.

No matter what.

10

RUMOUR HAS IT

"Susannah!"

I turned to see AJ waving at me from outside a café on Emerson Street. I smiled and made my way over to her and her brother Anders, who greeted me with an unenthusiastic nod. He was sitting in a wheelchair, one leg stretched out in front of him in a heavy cast, and he looked tired. The sun was beating down relentlessly as the heatwave we were experiencing showed no signs of stopping. Anders shifted uncomfortably in the wheelchair as I sat down next to AJ with a smile.

"Hi, how's it going?"

"Not bad, not bad. Just ignore Grumpy McGee over there," she told me firmly. "He's having a bad day."

Anders shot her a dirty look. "Do you wanna swap places?"

"Nope. And no matter how many times you ask me that, my answer's not gonna change. If you're going to sit there sulking, I'm going to ignore you and talk to someone I actually like. So," AJ said, turning to face me. "What brings you out into this booming metropolis?"

I looked around us at the nikau palms that lined the brick-paved street, which shimmered under the buffeting heat. Napier, the art deco capital of New Zealand. A rather dubious claim to fame, but one that the city has long been proud of. The annual festival was coming up, and would bring an influx of tourists into the region. But for now, it was still fairly quiet on the main streets.

"Shopping," I told AJ. "Well, trying to, anyway. I'm not having much luck."

She stirred the remnants of her iced coffee with her straw, and raised her eyebrows at me. "Shopping for what?"

"A dress," I admitted. "I've got this party that I'm supposed to be going to tonight, and I realised this morning that I have nothing to wear."

AJ couldn't stop her eyes from reflexively scanning me, her expression dubious. "Really? But you always have the nicest clothes."

I felt myself blush as Anders turned his head to look at me as well. "Riding clothes, sure. Party clothes, not so much."

"Well I'm not sure AJ is your go-to advice person for party clothes," Anders informed me. "I don't think she's ever seen a dress in her life, let alone put one on." AJ lifted the straw out of her iced coffee and flicked it in his direction. A glob of whipped cream landed on his cheek, but he just wiped it off and licked it from his finger before continuing to talk to me. "Whose party is it?"

"Callie Taylor's."

He frowned for a moment, then shook his head. "Don't know her."

AJ feigned astonishment. "Someone in the Hawke's Bay that you don't know? Alert the media."

"Just because you don't have any friends outside of that pony of yours," Anders replied, his mood lightening as we spoke. "Don't judge people for their choices."

"I'm not judging *people*," AJ told him. "Just you."

"It doesn't really matter," I said, trying to get them back on track. "I might not go anyway. I've got the vet coming at three, so it kind of depends on what she says about Buck whether I'll even be in the mood."

"Oh right!" AJ said guiltily, giving me an anxious look. "How's he doing?"

I shrugged, the thought of Buck taking some of the shine off the day. "He's improving, but slowly. We're still not sure what caused any of it, or whether he'll ever be able to be ridden again." I didn't say anything about strangles. I was terrified to even mention it in case word spread, and people started blaming me for starting an epidemic. The first swab test had come back terrifyingly inconclusive, and the results of the second one were still a few days away.

"That sucks, I'm sorry," AJ said commiseratively.

She sucked the last remnants of her drink up the straw noisily, and Anders rolled his eyes at me, cracking a small smile. Despite my mood, I smiled back at him. I couldn't blame Katy for having a crush on him, no matter how much it irritated AJ that her best friend was into her brother. He really was gorgeous, and he seemed like a nice guy.

But then, didn't they all?

"Hey, it's Anders!"

Our heads all swivelled to see a pair of pretty teenage girls coming in our direction, their focus riveted on AJ's older brother. They completely ignored me and AJ as they seated themselves around Anders and started chattering to him as though we weren't even there.

I raised my eyebrows at AJ, who pulled a face. "Can't take him anywhere," she said ruefully. "It's what happens when you have too many friends."

"I wouldn't know," I admitted, glancing back at the girls, who were sitting as close to Anders as possible and unabashedly flirting with him. I was still in two minds over whether to go to Callie's party tonight. It was so far outside of my comfort zone, but if I wanted to make new friends, I had to put myself out there. Right?

"Hey, can I ask you something?"

I looked back at AJ. "Sure."

She leaned across the table towards me, lowering her voice. Her expression was serious, and I had a prickling sense of foreboding even before she spoke. "Is it true about you and Connor?"

Despite the stifling heat of the day, a cold sweat broke over my skin at the mention of his name. More than anything, I wished I could stop myself reacting that way.

"Is what true, exactly?" I was relieved that my voice sounded calm and didn't betray my emotions.

"It's just something that Katy said that Anna told her." AJ looked a little embarrassed to be repeating third-hand information, but she was clearly very curious. "That you hooked up with Connor at Nationals."

"What's it to you if I did?" The words escaped before I could even consider what I was saying. Maybe I should've denied it – did anyone know, other than the two of us? Well, obviously Anna knew. Or did she? My head was spinning, and I fought hard to maintain my outward calm.

AJ looked taken aback. "Nothing, I just… Anna was just riled up about it, that's all. And Katy said she was being ridiculous, because Connor, well because he hates you, that's what she said anyway. But I kept thinking about how awkward things got when he turned up at Katy's truck at Taihape and I just wondered, that's all. I'm sorry, I'm being nosy. It's a flaw."

I glanced over at Anders, still being drooled over by the group of now four girls who surrounded him. How come he was that good-looking and still seemed like a decent guy, when someone like Connor was only about half as attractive but went around acting like he was God's gift to the universe?

"What's it got to do with Anna, anyway?" I clutched at that straw, hoping to deflect the conversation onto someone else before I ended up spilling the beans.

"Apparently she's had a thing going with Connor for a while," AJ said conspiratorially, leaning forward and talking quickly, relishing the opportunity to gossip. "They've been hooking up in secret at all the shows, but he ditched her at Nationals and disappeared, and then he said you'd been all over him, and…"

I cut her off there, my anger rising. "First of all, *he* was the one who was all over *me*. And second, she can keep him." I stood up, my legs shaking under me. "I have to go."

AJ stood up too, looking concerned. Anders and his friends were staring at us now, but I didn't care. Let them look. AJ stepped closer and lowered her voice.

"I'm sorry, I didn't mean to upset you. I just thought you should know that there are some rumours going around, that's all."

My throat was dry and sticky. "What rumours?"

"Well…" AJ avoided eye contact with me, staring at my shoulder as she spoke. "That you slept with him and now you keep texting him all the time, and trying to hook up with him again. Which *obviously* isn't true," she added, glancing up and catching the look on my face. "But I thought I should tell you what people are saying." I could tell by her expression that she was regretting saying anything.

I was regretting hearing it. My jaw was clenched so tight that it hurt, but I couldn't force it to relax. I took a breath, tried to stay calm.

"Of course it's not true. And you can tell Anna that I wouldn't touch Connor again with a ten foot pole. She's welcome to him, if she's dumb enough to want him."

AJ put her hand on my upper arm, looking worried. "Is everything okay? Did something –"

I cut her off before she could ask that question. I didn't want to lie, and I didn't want to talk about it. Certainly not in the middle of a crowded street.

"I'm fine," I told her. "Just came to my senses, that's all. And I really have to go. I've got the vet coming, so…"

"Yeah, of course. Take care of yourself." AJ looked like she wanted to hug me, but I stepped back, building my walls back up. I didn't want to cry in public, and I was scarily close to it just then.

"How's our patient doing?"

I put a hand on Buck's neck as Lesley strode towards us across the brittle grass. It still hadn't rained, and the unusually hot weather had gone beyond being a novelty and was rapidly turning into a drought.

"He's okay," I told Lesley when she reached my side. "Seems to be getting better in the evenings, but he's worse during the day."

"He won't be loving the heat," she agreed, setting her kit down at her feet and holding out a hand to Buck to sniff.

He obliged, his ears pricked warmly forward as he greeted her like an old friend. Despite the needles she'd stuck into his neck and the tubes she'd slid down his nostrils these past few days, he didn't hold a grudge. I counted myself lucky to have a pony as forgiving as him.

Lesley threaded her stethoscope into her ears and listened to Buck's heartbeat as he breathed in and out. His sides expanded and contracted heavily, and I watched with a concerned frown, counting his breaths.

"Heartrate is down to forty-two, which is an improvement," she told me. "I don't suppose you know his regular resting heartrate?" I shook my head. "Probably a good thing to check out with your other ponies. Resting heartrates can vary greatly between horses."

"Anything from twenty-eight to forty beats per minute," I said.

"That's right. Learn your ponies' resting heart rates, then you'll be able to keep an eye on any changes more easily. You know where to take a pulse?"

I nodded, placing two fingers against the artery under Buck's jaw.

"That's the one. You learn that at Pony Club?"

I shook my head. I'd never been to Pony Club – my parents had considered it to be beneath us. "No. I just…learned it. From books and YouTube and stuff." I shrugged under her curious expression. "I wanted to be a vet for a while."

Her eyebrows lifted. "Not anymore?"

"I'm not sure," I replied. "Sounds like it's a lot of work."

"Can't deny that," Lesley agreed. "Competitive to get into, hard work while you're studying and even harder once you're in practice. But it's incredibly rewarding. You should consider it."

"Maybe." I watched as she put the stethoscope buds back into her ears and started listening to Buck's lungs. She took her time, shifting the end of the stethoscope back and forth across his ribs and at the base of his trachea, then looked at me. "Want a listen?"

"Um, sure." I took the hot pink stethoscope from her and inserted the buds into my ears. Lesley took Buck's lead rope and stroked his head gently. "Where do I listen?"

"Between the ribs is the best place." She reached over and guided my hand, placing it halfway along Buck's ribcage. "Start there. Tell me what you hear."

It was fascinating, listening to the breath going in and out of Buck's lungs as I watched his sides move. I listened carefully, moving the stethoscope once or twice across his ribcage, then lower.

"Not too far back there," Lesley corrected me. "You'll end up listening to gut function. Lungs don't go beyond the last rib."

"Right." I pulled the earbuds from my ears and handed the stethoscope back to her. "Thanks."

"Hear anything interesting?"

I thought for a moment. "It sounded like he's wheezing a bit." She nodded, but my insight wasn't exactly revolutionary. In the middle of the day, when Buck's symptoms were the worst, he wheezed audibly. "But I didn't hear any crackling or anything like that," I added. I'd been doing some internet research, and had been warned to watch out for those kind of sounds.

"Right you are." Lesley went around to the other side of Buck and listened to his lungs again for a while before removing the stethoscope and slinging it around her neck. "His lungs are still battling, but he's showing some improvement. Heart rate and respiration are down, and his gums are a good colour."

"Capillary refill is normal, and so is his temperature," I told her, and she grinned at me.

"You barely even need me," she said cheerfully. "You're doing a great job. And is he coughing less?"

"A bit less, but he's still quite bad." As if he knew what we were saying, Buck dropped his head and coughed heavily a couple of times.

"Hmm. What're you feeding him?"

"Soaked hay, and damp grain with beet pulp twice a day. I'd give him more but I don't want him getting too fat," I told her, looking at Buck's rounded sides. He'd already eaten the grass down on the lawn, and Mum was getting increasingly irritated about it.

"You ever hear of a hay steamer?" I shook my head, and Lesley continued as she rummaged around in her kit. "You might want to look into that. There's a company here that sells them, and they work well. It'll kill any mould spores and is more palatable than soaked hay."

"Okay." I rubbed Buck's nose as she straightened up and looked around.

"Where is your hay?"

"In the barn."

"Show me."

I unclipped Buck's rope and left him on the lawn, Lesley following right behind as we made our way to the barn. The double doors at the front were rolled back, and I walked down the aisle past our loose boxes and tack room, then stopped at the far end, where the hay was stacked tightly, floor to ceiling.

Lesley went straight to the open bale sitting at the front of the stack, and tore it apart in the middle, inspecting the hay closely.

"Smells all right," she conceded, looking around. "Is this first or second cut?"

"First," I told her. "We used to get second cut from down the road, but Dad got talking to a farmer at the feed store who swore his first cut was the best. Cost more than the other stuff we used to get, but it's top quality hay."

"So this hay's from a new supplier? When did you get it in?"

"Uh…a few days before we left for Nationals." Why hadn't I thought of mentioning that before? "D'you think the hay's the problem?"

"It might be. Might not."

Lesley tore a biscuit out of the bale and carried it back down the aisle into the daylight. I followed her curiously and watched as she tore it apart and shook it. A fine dust lifted from the biscuit as pieces of hay cascaded to the ground at her feet.

"It's dusty," I said quietly, watching the dust particles float around us.

Lesley nodded. "It's not the worst," she told me. "It's not bad hay, but it's got a lot of leaf shatter." She caught my confused expression and clarified. "See here, where the leafy parts of the grass are breaking up into small particles? That can happen when the hay is raked and baled when it's too dry. It's tough, in a dry summer like this, to avoid dusty hay, but it can be done."

"How?"

"Look at the paddocks you're buying hay from before you agree to purchase it. Be especially wary of hay paddocks that border dirt roads that get a lot of traffic. They kick the dust up something shocking, and if there's any kind of breeze, it ends up on the paddocks and gets baled, especially if the hay has already been cut."

"Okay. So we should get rid of this stuff?" I hated to think what Dad was going to say when I told him we had to replenish our entire hay stock.

"I wouldn't keep feeding it to Buck, even soaked or steamed, if you can avoid it. Are your other ponies okay with it?"

I started to nod, then paused. "Skip was coughing yesterday when I rode him. Only once or twice though, and he seemed fine otherwise. But I'd given him some hay to munch on while I tacked him up," I remembered. "I didn't soak it first, because I didn't think I needed to."

"I'd say that answers your question then," she told me. "Like I said, it's not bad hay, and for the majority of horses it won't cause them a problem, especially if it's fed out on a paddock where it can be spread around and the dust can escape. But I'd avoid feeding it to stabled horses unless it was well-soaked first." She tossed the torn biscuit onto the grass behind us. "And I always recommend storing hay in a separate building from your stables. Even the best hay is going to release dust particles. If you need to stable Buck, use straw or thick shavings – never sawdust. But I'd avoid stabling him altogether, if you can."

"Even in winter?" I asked dubiously. "He's not really the rough and tumble type."

Buck liked his creature comforts – he was always the first to the gate to be caught when it was raining, and he thought being left outside in the bad weather was a form of cruel and unusual punishment. The lightest shower made him shiver if he didn't have a cover on, and he detested getting rain in his eyes.

She smiled at me. "He's tougher than he looks, I promise. If you're really worried, build him a three-sided shelter in one of the paddocks that he can get into to avoid the rain."

"He won't like being left outside by himself," I said with a sigh, and Buck took his cue from me and decided to whinny to Skip, who replied throatily. Forbes joined in half-heartedly, but it was Buck and Skip who were the most attached to each other.

Lesley walked around the back of the barn and looked at the ponies in the paddock. Forbes was grazing again, preoccupied as usual by food, but Skip had his head high and was staring in Buck's direction. The dark bay pony was just visible through the trees, and I watched him force out another rattling neigh.

"Might be time to move him closer to his buddies," Lesley said as she started walking back to her ute. "He should still be isolated, just in case, but it won't do him much good to be stressing about it." She stopped and looked behind us, scanning the row of paddocks. "Maybe you could fence him off a section over there, under the trees so he has plenty of shade. In the meantime, here. Start putting this in his feed twice a day. I'll write out the dosage."

Lesley sat down on the grass and pulled out a pen and notepad as I examined the container of medicine in my hand. "It's a bronchodilator," she told me. "Give him a go on that. If he doesn't improve enough, we can try him on an inhaler."

"Okay. Thanks."

"No worries." She got to her feet and dusted the dry grass off her butt. "I'd better get moving. Lots more patients to see today." She picked up her kit and looked at me. "Oh, and if you ever decide that you want to pursue that vet career, let me know. I'd be happy to help you out if I can."

I blinked at her. "Really?"

She nodded. "Yeah, why not? You're a smart girl who cares about animals." She took a couple of steps, then turned back. "As long as you get into it for the right reasons. It's not a career for someone who's afraid of hard work."

I blushed at the reminder of my earlier excuse. "I'm not really," I told her, and she grinned.

"That's what I figured. If it's what you really want, go for it. Don't let anyone talk you out of your dreams."

I watched Lesley walk away towards her ute in the blistering heat. Her jeans and boots were dusty, her shirt was creased and worn, and her heavy ponytail had left a damp patch between her shoulderblades. Her knuckles were bruised and her palms calloused and her skin was weather-worn, but she knew exactly who she was. She hadn't been afraid to stand up to my father, and she'd just told me exactly what I needed to hear.

If I could end up being anything like her, I decided as I went to tidy up the discarded biscuit of hay, I might be able to consider myself a success.

11

PARTY TIME

"You made it! Wait, what are you wearing?"

Callie looked me up and down disparagingly, and I felt my self-confidence ebb again. I'd spent ages getting dressed, trying to find something appropriate for a party like this, and in the end had settled on skinny jeans, strappy sandals and a cream sleeveless top made of quality silk. I'd brushed my hair out and added a small amount of jewellery, then spent about half an hour applying enough makeup to look like I'd made an effort, but not so much that Dad wouldn't let me out of the house. He'd just dropped me off, and I'd only just managed to get out of the car without him accompanying me to the door to meet Callie's parents. Which was looking like a good thing, since they were nowhere in sight.

"I…" I didn't know what to say.

Callie leaned against the door frame, her dark blue dress clinging to every curve on her body, and shook her head at me.

"You know that this is a *Valentine's Day* party, not a Sunday school party, right?" she told me, her disappointment in me clear.

Two of Callie's friends appeared in the hallway behind her, both dressed in short, tight dresses, one with hair half-straightened, the other with hair half-curled. They looked at me and Sabrina raised a heavily-plucked eyebrow.

"I hope you brought a change of clothes with you."

I flushed as they all looked around for evidence, and shook my

135

head. "It's not my fault, okay?" I told them, placing the blame where I could. "My dad wouldn't let me out of the house wearing anything other than this."

"Well then," Callie said, her expression brightening as she opened the front door wider and motioned me in. "It's a good thing you're here early, because I've got a wardrobe full of dresses that are going to look amazing on you!"

Half an hour later, I stood in front of the full-length mirror and stared at my unfamiliar reflection. The short red dress barely reached the middle of my thigh, and was cut low in front, showing off an unprecedented amount of cleavage. Callie had dragged me straight to her bedroom and proceeded to fling an array of dresses at me to try on, and this one had been declared the unanimous winner. Everyone loved it – except me.

It looked good, I couldn't deny that. But it made a statement that I wasn't sure I wanted to make. There was nothing subtle about this dress.

"You're going to have guys all over you tonight," Sabrina declared, beaming at me as though that's all I could possibly hope for. I felt my skin crawl, but forced myself to smile as she ushered me over to the bed and sat me down, then proceeded to apply more makeup to my eyes, my cheeks, my lips.

"There," she said a few minutes later. "Man, I don't know if you should've invited this one along, Callie."

Callie turned around, mascara brush in one hand, her eyes already blackened with eyeliner. "Why not?" She looked at me, and grinned. "Damn, girl. You're gonna knock 'em dead tonight. Aren't you glad we made you change?"

I looked at my clothes, tossed unceremoniously into the corner of the room. I wished I was still wearing them, that I hadn't let Callie and her friends push me so far outside of my comfort zone.

Stop it, I told myself. *You wanted more friends, here they are. Just go with it. Step outside your comfort zone for once.*

"Drink time!"

I looked up to see Jaime standing in front of me, holding out a glass of pale pink liquid.

"No thanks."

Jaime rolled her eyes in Callie's direction, and Callie laughed. "It's fine," she told me. "There's no alcohol in it."

I wasn't sure whether I believed her, but I didn't want to accuse her of lying in front of her friends. I took the glass from Jaime and looked over at Callie.

"Are your parents home?"

"Yeah, why?"

I shrugged, and took a sip of the drink. To my relief, I couldn't taste any alcohol. "Just wondering. I haven't seen them."

"They know better than to get in our way," Callie said dismissively, then raised her glass to us. "Here's to a night we'll never forget!"

The music was thumping, a steady beat that throbbed through my head and made me feel dizzy. If there truly hadn't been any alcohol in that first drink, I was certain that there had been in the next two. But drinking punch had given me something to do, at least. I'd drained my third glass a few minutes ago, and sat on the edge of the couch, twirling the thin stem of the punch glass between my fingers while Sabrina let some guy feel her up on the couch next to me.

"Hi."

He was standing next to the couch and grinning down at me. I smiled back, wishing I hadn't let Callie talk me into wearing such a low-cut dress. This guy, whoever he was, had a prime view right down the front of it, and I tugged at the thin shoulder straps reflexively.

He kept grinning, but held his hand out towards me. "Wanna refill?"

"Oh, no. I'm fine."

"Yeah you are." I cringed, but he didn't seem to realise what a corny line that was. "I'm Declan, by the way."

He sat down on the wide arm of the couch and leaned against the wall behind us, continuing to smile down at me.

"I'm Susannah."

"How do you know Callie?" He took a swig from the can in his hand, and I could smell the bourbon on his breath.

"We go to school together." My eyes ranged around the room, looking for Callie, but I couldn't see her. There were so many people here, crammed together into the large rumpus room at the bottom of Callie's house. She'd ushered everyone in here as they arrived and shut the door firmly behind us, explaining that the room was soundproof, and that her parents didn't want to be disturbed.

Sabrina was engaged in a full-on make-out session now, and she fell back against my shoulder as the guy she was with continued his exploration of her throat with his tongue. I elbowed her in the back, and she broke off the kiss.

"Sorry." She giggled. "Jack, would you let me sit up?"

"Why don't you two get a room?" Declan suggested, shifting from the arm of the couch to stand over Sabrina and her new friend instead. "Go on, get out of here, stop crushing my new friend Hannah."

"Susannah," I corrected him, but I don't think he heard me over the loud music. Jack stood up and grabbed Sabrina's hand, pulling her to her feet behind him.

"Come on then, let's give Dec some space," Jack said, grinning down at me with a gleam in his eye before slapping Declan on the shoulder. "Good luck, mate."

"Cheers." Declan toasted his friend, then dropped down onto the couch next to me. "Now, where were we?"

He wasn't a bad-looking guy. He could've used a haircut, he had a smattering of acne across one cheek and an earring in one ear that looked slightly ridiculous, but overall he was fairly appealing. *Give him a chance,* I told myself. So I smiled, and shrugged, peering at him through the several coats of mascara that Sabrina had applied to my eyelashes.

"I think we were just about to start talking about the weather," I said.

"What?" The music was loud, drowning out my feeble attempt at conversation. I shrugged again, and lifted my glass to sip at my drink, then realised that the glass was still empty. I looked at Declan to see if he'd offer again to go get me another one, but he was too preoccupied with staring at my chest. I waved the empty glass in front of his eye line, and he snapped his attention back to my face with a sheepish grin.

"Sorry. Got distracted." He shuffled closer to me on the couch, and turned to face me. "That dress is just…wow."

"Thanks." I tugged self-consciously at the hemline that was riding up my thigh, which only served to draw his attention to it. "It's not mine, it's Callie's."

"Well it looks great on you. Better than it does on her, I bet."

Declan stretched one arm out over the back of the couch and grinned. I leaned back slightly, trying to put some space between us, but the arm of the couch held me in place. I glanced around the room, my eyes catching on Callie as she sauntered past with one boy on either side of her, both of them practically tripping over themselves to get her attention. She noticed me and grinned, glancing at Declan then shooting me a thumbs-up as she continued on her way, disappearing towards the back corner of the room.

Declan shifted closer again, his body leaning up against me. The pressure of his weight against my side made my skin prickle. The smell of the bourbon combined with his liberally-applied deodorant made my nostrils burn. Then his hand was on the back of my head, and he was leaning in towards me and his lips were millimetres from mine.

I leaned back, trying to smile to lighten the mood. "Easy tiger. We only just met."

He was still grinning, leaning in closer as I pulled away. "What can I say? You're driving me wild."

Then he went in for the kiss, and I was up against the arm of the couch with nowhere left to go. He had one hand on my thigh, sliding up underneath my dress, and I grabbed his wrist and pushed it away.

"Stop it!"

The music thumped on around us in a relentless rhythm, mimicking my racing heartbeat.

"What?" He feigned confusion, but he let me move his hand away. I knew I had to get out of this situation, but my limbs felt heavy and I couldn't get my body to cooperate. Shit. How much had I had to drink?

Declan leaned back against the couch and glared at me as though I'd just ruined his night. In his mind, I probably had. "You a lesbian or something?"

I glared right back at him. "What? No."

"Then what's your problem?" He lunged in towards me for another kiss, but I'd had enough. My anger and fear and confusion all collided with each other, and I retaliated by slapping him across the cheek with as much force as I could muster.

"My *problem*," I told him loudly, "is that you're an asshole!"

The music that had been so insistent for the past hour suddenly took a break, letting everyone in the room hear exactly what I'd just said. They all turned and stared at me, and I made a concerted effort to stand up, pushing myself to the edge of the couch and getting to my feet.

Declan was swearing at me, one hand pressed against his cheek as he called me crazy amongst other things. A few people had gathered around us, but they mostly seemed amused by the fact that Declan had been slapped than by what had upset me.

My head was spinning, and I was eternally grateful that I had chosen to stick to my own sandals rather than the teetering heels that Callie had tried to talk me into wearing.

The thumping music was back, and as I stood there, trying to work out just how drunk I was and what I should do next, Callie appeared next to me.

"Susannah." She put a hand on my shoulder, and I turned to face her in relief. She'd get me out of the situation. That's what friends are for, right? But she was looking at me with a disappointed expression. "I think you should go home."

I blinked at her in disbelief. "What?"

"You've had too much to drink," she told me, her own voice slurred slightly. God, what had been in that punch? "It's probably for the best if you go home and sleep it off. We wouldn't want you to do anything that you'll regret."

I opened my mouth to say something, but she just squeezed my shoulder and then turned away. Declan was still sitting on the couch, leering at me. He'd won that round, and he knew it. My hands were shaking as I reached over and picked up the small bag that I'd been carrying all night, the one that had my cell phone in it. Instinct had dictated that I kept it with me, and I'd never been more grateful for that decision. Declan said something as I leaned towards him, getting one last good look down the front of the red dress as I restrained the urge to beat him around the head with my bag before I straightened up and walked away with as much dignity as I could muster.

Outside, the air was cool. I walked across the dimly-lit garden towards the road, stopping at the mailbox and looking up the street. I was a long way from home, and I didn't have any money to call a taxi. I toyed with the idea of calling one and then getting Dad to pay when he dropped me home, but I already knew how well that'd go down. So I did the one thing that was almost unthinkable, because I was completely out of options.

The phone rang, and rang, and rang. Finally, just as I was starting to give up hope and think I was going to have to call a taxi anyway, the line clicked.

"Hello?"

"Hi. It's me." *Sound sober.*

I could hear the frown in my father's voice. "Susie? What's wrong?"

"Can you come pick me up?"

"What happened?"

"Nothing." As if I was going to tell him. He'd lock me in the house and never let me leave again. Although right now, that didn't seem like such a bad idea. "I'm just sick of this party, okay?"

I heard him sigh. "I'll be there in ten minutes."

"Okay. Thanks."

I hung up the phone, then looked around for somewhere to sit down. There was a large boulder at the front of the Taylors' driveway, and I sank down onto that. The red dress rode up my thigh, and I tugged at it savagely. The facts slowly sank in as I sat there in the moonlight. My dad was coming to pick me up, and I was dressed like this. For a moment I considered doing nothing, and damn the consequences, but I already knew that I couldn't afford to make things worse. So I stood up again, and made my way back towards the house.

I headed for the front door, wanting to avoid the party downstairs. It would only take a few steps to get down the hall, up the stairs and into Callie's bedroom, where I could change back into my own clothes. The desire to get out of this tight, clinging dress was overpowering, and I gripped the front door handle tightly when I got to it and twisted it hard.

Nothing happened. I tried again, but still nothing. It was locked, I realised belatedly. There was a doorbell right next to it, and after a moment's hesitation, I pressed it. Within the house, I heard it chime. Callie was right about the rumpus room being soundproof. I could still feel the vibrations thudding through the ground from the heavy bass, but the music itself was muted, barely audible.

I shifted my weight impatiently, and checked the time on my phone. Almost five minutes had already passed since I'd spoken to my Dad. I rang the doorbell again, holding my finger down for a couple of seconds. Then footsteps finally came towards the door, and it opened.

A tall blonde woman stared down at me, looking annoyed. "The party's downstairs," she said, starting to close the door again.

"I know. I'm going home early, but first I need to go up to Callie's room and get my things."

She frowned, then huffed out an impatient sigh. "Hurry up then. You're supposed to stay downstairs," she repeated as I slipped past her into the hallway. "We told Callie that we didn't want her friends traipsing through the house at all hours."

I just stared at her, trying to find words. "I won't be a second," I managed to say. "My dad's picking me up in a couple of minutes. I just need to get my things."

"Hurry up then."

I made my way up the stairs and stopped on the landing, looking around. Which room was Callie's? I knew it looked out towards the ocean, but it was too dark now to tell which way the ocean was, and I was completely disoriented. I walked across the landing and opened the nearest door to find myself staring into what must be her parents' bedroom. A huge bed in the middle of the room, with floor to ceiling windows on two sides. I shut the door behind me, and went to the next one. That was a bathroom, and I was getting frantic as time ticked by. What if Dad arrived and I wasn't at the gate? Would he come up and knock on the door? I really didn't want him getting into a scrap with Callie's parents, and I flung open the door of the next room in desperation.

This was it. I recognised the shape of the room, the location of the window, the clothes scattered across the carpet. I reached for the light switch and flipped it on, focusing on the far corner where I knew my clothes lay discarded.

"What the hell?!"

I jumped, my heart leaping as I realised the room wasn't empty. There were two people in the bed, under the covers, glaring at me furiously.

"Sorry!" I apologised quickly, feeling more awkward than I had all night, which considering how the night had gone so far, was pretty incredible. "I just came to get my things, they're just over…"

"Turn the light off and get outta here!" the guy snapped, and as he pulled the covers up higher, I recognised Jack. I wondered if Callie knew that Sabrina was here with him, in her bed. Not that it was any of my business, but gross. I flipped the light back off and stood there for a second, unsure of what to do. Did I go and get my clothes, or leave them and get out of there?

Jack made the decision for me by telling me to get lost, only he didn't use those exact words. Defeated, I stepped back out into the hallway and pulled the door closed behind me, wondering what I was supposed to do next. There was an ugly painting of a horse on the wall opposite me, one of those modern art pieces that looked like someone who had only seen a horse once in their life had painted it. The horse was painted a metallic gold, and it was rearing on wonky hind legs, rolling one eye at me. Maybe the artist had been going for a depiction of power or strength, but all I could think as I stared at it was that with hocks like that, the horse wouldn't have a sound day in its life.

I shook my head, trying to refocus my thoughts. I wanted to go home and see my ponies. I wanted to go check on Buck, who was now in his new paddock under the trees, within sight of the other two. I'd set it up for him that afternoon, as soon as Lesley had left. I should've just stayed home with him. Should never have come to this stupid party. Should've known I wouldn't fit in.

I stood up straight and headed back towards the stairs, abandoning my clothes to their fate. I had to get back to the gate before Dad arrived. I went down the stairs as fast as I could, feeling more sober by the second as I stepped into the hall and went back to the front door. Callie's mother had disappeared back into the living room, and I pulled the door open and stepped back out into the evening air.

I was just in time. Dad drove up as I reached the end of the driveway, and I hurried over to him and slid gratefully onto the cool leather seat of his Audi. I could feel my father's eyes on me as the car door snicked shut behind me, so I stared straight ahead at the streetlights, avoiding his glare.

"What the *hell* are you wearing?"

"Can we not do this right now?" I asked.

But Dad shifted the car into park, and rested his hands on the steering wheel. "I think now is the perfect time." He sniffed the air, his frown deepening. "Have you been drinking?"

I closed my eyes, not trusting myself to speak.

"I'm talking to you, Susannah."

"I know. I can hear you."

"What do you have to say for yourself?"

I took a breath, then let it out again. "Can we just go home? Please?" I heard my voice crack on the last word, and felt the atmosphere in the car recede slightly. My eye were still shut tight, but I heard Dad moving the gear shift, and the car glided into motion.

"Don't think this is the end of this conversation."

I was under no such illusion. Nothing was ever over until my father had had the last word. But I didn't want to deal with it right now, so I kept my eyes closed and said nothing.

When we got home, I went straight to my room and peeled the red dress off, then kicked it across the room. It lay slumped in the corner as I changed into pyjama shorts and a t-shirt, feeling at once more comfortable in my own skin. I went into the ensuite and looked at myself in the mirror. No wonder Dad had flipped out when he'd seen me. My eyes were black smudges against my pale skin, and I turned the hot water on and grabbed a flannel, scrubbing at my face and eyes until I'd removed every last trace of makeup. My eyes were bloodshot and stinging, but I felt like myself again.

There was a rap at my bedroom door, and then I heard Mum's voice. "You in here Susie?"

I shut off the tap and went back out into my room, trying to appear composed. "I'm here."

Mum looked at me curiously. "Your father is very unhappy with you."

"I know."

I sat down on the end of my bed, bare toes digging into the deep carpet. I waited for Mum to come into my room, to sit down and put an arm around me and ask me what was wrong. Why I'd come home so early. How I could've let myself get peer pressured into wearing things I didn't want to wear, into drinking when I'd promised I wouldn't.

But she didn't. "He's going to have to let you grow up sometime."

I looked up at her, registering slowly that she was dressed for dinner in a floaty blouse and pencil skirt. "Where have you been?"

"Out with clients." She didn't quite meet my eyes as she spoke. "I've got some very exciting projects coming up." She seemed happy, caught up in her own world, oblivious to mine.

"That's good." What else could I say?

"Your father doesn't like that either, but he's going to have to realise that he can't control us," Mum said, straightening up and drawing her shoulders back. "We've got to take our lives back, Susannah, and not let him push us around anymore."

"Are you going to leave him?" The words came out before I could stop them. I supposed I was still slightly drunk.

Mum flinched, her eyes shooting to the far corner of my room as she denied it. "Of course not. Don't be ridiculous. It's just a rough patch." She tapped her fingernails against the doorframe, then sighed. "Anyway, it's late. Time for bed."

I stood up. "I'm going to check on Buck."

She almost said no, almost put her foot down and told me that it was late, and that I was to do as I was told. Truth be told, I almost wanted her to. The mother that I knew, the mother I'd grown up with, would have.

But she didn't.

"Of course." She stepped back onto the landing. "Just don't be too late, okay?"

"Okay."

As I made my way slowly downstairs, the phone rang. I was sitting down and pulling my paddock boots on at the front door when I heard Dad answer it in his office.

"Hello?" A pause, then a snarky response. "Yes, of course it's Derrick, who else would it be?"

Some lucky person was about to bear the brunt of my father's anger with me. I stood up quickly, and my hand was on the door handle when he spoke again.

"And there's no doubt this time? Nothing *inconclusive* about this result?"

I froze, the blood pumping frantically through my veins as I realised who he was talking to, and what he was talking about.

My father's next words confirmed it. "Well, good. I'll let Susie know that he's got the all clear." Another pause, then two words I never thought I'd hear my father say. "Thanks, Lesley."

I no longer cared how mad he was at me, or whether he was going to give me hell. I stuck my head through the half-open door into his office and Dad looked up, his expression softer and more relaxed than it had been in weeks as he hung up the phone.

"That was the vet."

"I heard. It's not strangles?"

"Definitively not. Which we knew all along, really," Dad said, as though we actually had known and hadn't just hoped. "But it's now official."

I felt as though I could breathe again after holding my breath for weeks. I let my face relax into a smile, and my father smiled back at me. I rested my head against the door frame and took a deep breath.

"That's awesome."

"Lesley's coming over in the morning to get him started on a course of antibiotics. Since he's improved with a change of feed and environment, and it hasn't spread to the others, she thinks it's allergic. I've got that hay steamer ordered."

"Thanks." I smiled at him again. Maybe today wasn't a complete disaster after all. "I'm gonna go tell Buck the good news."

Buck was snoozing, lying down under the big totara in the corner of the paddock. I walked over to him, picking my way across the dry ground in the pale moonlight.

"Hey buddy." He lifted his head and pricked his ears, watching me approach. "How you doing?"

Buck whiffled his nostrils at me as I reached his side, and I gave him the piece of carrot that I'd swiped out of the kitchen on my way down here. He crunched it cheerfully, eyeing me up as I sat down next to him. His breathing was more regular, and I couldn't hear any wheezing.

"We'll get you that hay steamer," I told him. "Dad's already ordered it, and a whole new load of hay." I reached up and ran my fingers through his thick forelock. "You're going to be fine. I'll take care of you, okay? I promise."

Buck sighed and rested his chin on the ground at my feet, half-closing his eyes. I sat with him, watching his sides move in and out with each slow breath, overcome with relief.

12

KEEP MOVING FORWARD

Forbes tossed his head as I closed my leg and pushed him into the contact, ignoring the small temper tantrum he was having. Bruce stood in the middle of the arena, watching us carefully as he leaned back against a jump stand. The heat of the midday sun baked up off the arena surface, and Forbes's shoulders were drenched in sweat.

"Keep your leg there, don't let him argue," Bruce coached as I circled the dark bay pony around him. "He's got to learn that he can't just toss his toys and refuse to work."

Forbes gave in for a few strides and flexed his jaw, lowering his head and releasing his hold against my hand. "That's better. When he softens to you, you soften a little to him," Bruce reminded me. "But soften from the elbow, not the hand!"

I closed my fingers around the reins again as I struggled to break that bad habit. When I'd started taking lessons with Bruce two years ago, he'd told me in no uncertain terms that I had very hard, unforgiving hands and that I needed to learn to give as well as take. He'd sent me to a dressage trainer for a few months to learn the 'basics' before he'd coach me over fences. I'd been mortified, but I'd taken his advice, and had made steady progress since under his guidance. But I'd become so self-conscious about my 'hard hands' that I now had developed the opposite problem – a tendency to open my hand too much and give away too much contact – and Forbes took full advantage.

It still amazed me, sometimes, how much I still had to learn about riding – and how little I'd known for so long. I wished I could go back through the years and do things over. I still felt guilty when I thought about the ponies who'd put up with me for so long, and how hard I'd made it for them. There was only so much I could do now to make up for my past mistakes, but I was determined to try.

"Get that pony moving forward!"

I nudged Forbes with my leg in an attempt to energise him, but he'd reached his limit of compliance for the day and threw in a big buck, trying to unseat me. I sat tight, lifting my hands to bring his head back up and pushing him forward again like Bruce was telling me to do, although mostly I was reacting by instinct and barely listening to my coach's shouts. Forbes tried another couple of half-hearted bucks, then gave in and trotted on.

But Bruce wasn't satisfied. "I know he's in a strop, but he needs to move out of that little shuffle he's got going on," he said. "That's not a proper trot, and he can't be allowed to get away with only giving you that when you've specifically asked for more."

I sat up taller, closed my leg again and pushed Forbes forward. He surged, and I corrected him with my reins, holding him together between hand and leg. For half a stride, I felt his back lift, felt his hindquarters start to engage, and got the small surge of adrenalin that always accompanied his powerful, ground-covering trot. But it didn't last. Forbes changed his mind abruptly about cooperating and slammed the brakes on, nearly sending me up his neck. I gritted my teeth and put my leg on again, but I knew what was coming.

Forbes tossed his head twice, then reared. I leaned forward, reaching my hands around his neck so I didn't interfere with his balance. He stood, poised, on his hind legs in a public declaration of his rebellion, then returned to all fours. I pushed him forward again, knowing through bitter experience that kicking or smacking him now would only cause him to rear higher. Bruce was swearing, and although I knew his expletives were directed at the pony and not me, it still made me tense up. I blocked him out and clicked my tongue to Forbes, the pressure from my legs still insistent against his sides.

Forbes took three steps in walk then reared again, a little higher this time. I could feel my temper boiling up inside me, but I knew I had to keep a lid on it. Losing my rag wasn't going to help the situation. Bruce was saying something, and I pushed my attention back to him.

"What?"

"Bring his head round to the left, then send him forward. He can't rear if he's not straight."

I followed Bruce's instructions, and to my surprise, discovered that he was right. I walked Forbes in a small circle, then brought him up to trot and made the circle a little larger. When he got bolshy and threatened to be naughty, I took him straight onto a smaller circle again until he capitulated.

"Better. Now, let's get that stronger trot out of him," Bruce insisted.

I closed my legs against Forbes's sides and sent him forward, and although he tossed his head irritably, he complied at last with my request and moved forward with a powerful, swinging stride. I moved him out to the outside track and worked him around the perimeter of the arena, changed the rein and went back the other way. The fight seemed to have gone out of Forbes, and he did as he was told, but his tail swished and his ears were laid back. He had no joy in what he was doing, and his reluctance, despite his outward appearance of cooperation, took the pleasure out of it for me too.

"Bring him back to walk, and give him a long rein. That'll do him for today," Bruce decided, to my relief. "He's learned he has to work when he's told, but he's tired and it's important to end on a successful note."

I drew Forbes back to a walk and let the reins out onto his sweating neck, giving him an appreciative pat.

"You handled that well," Bruce said as I circled the pony around him, letting his muscles relax as his body started to cool down. "When I first started teaching you, that would've been the beginning of the end."

I shrugged, slipping my feet out of my stirrups and stretching my legs. "If I still rode now like I did then, Forbes wouldn't even let me get on him."

"Probably true." He looked at the bay pony, who'd come to a halt to scratch his head on his foreleg. "Does he get much variety?"

I blinked at him, confused. "What do you mean?"

"I mean, do you hack him out much? Take him to the beach, ride him down the road? Does he get a change of scenery apart from when he goes to shows?"

I could feel my face flushing red. "Um, not really."

Bruce just looked at me, like he was waiting for me to say something else. I stared down at Forbes's neatly pulled mane, and ran a few strands of it through my fingers as my pony lifted his head again and sighed, resting a hind leg.

"Well I suggest that you start," he said eventually. "I don't know how much land you have here, but there's a big farm down the end of your road. I know the owners, and if you got in touch and asked nicely, I'm sure they'd let you ride through their place. Some hills would do him the world of good, get him thinking forward again."

I couldn't look at him, so I just kept staring down at Forbes's neck.

"Are you listening, or ignoring me?" Bruce asked irritably.

"I'm not allowed to ride on the road," I explained. "And the Cumberlands would never let me ride through their place."

Bruce frowned at me, opened his mouth in rebuttal, then stopped. I looked down at my pony again, at his sweat-soaked neck, and nudged him back into walk.

"Your old man pick a fight with them?"

I nodded. "Just like he does with everyone. We're only on speaking terms with one of our neighbours." And only because she was a nosy old cow who loved gossip as much as Mum did. Not out of any great love for any of us.

"Well, see if you can get your dad to truck you down to the beach once or twice at least," Bruce said, sounding slightly defeated. "Or ride this one around what land you do have. You can't school him all the time. He needs a change of scenery or he'll just turn sour and quit on you entirely."

"Okay."

"Shows don't count," Bruce warned me.

"Got it."

He walked towards me, and I halted Forbes again as Bruce pushed his sunglasses up onto his head and looked at me.

"Sorry about Ireland. I know you were hoping to be picked for the squad. You made first reserve, if that's any consolation."

I shrugged, but my heart lifted a little with that news. "Really?"

"Yeah. Well, there wasn't really any choice. It was very close between the top three candidates."

I wondered whether he was just saying that to make me feel better. Bruce looked over at the gate, where Dad would normally stand and watch. But he'd forgone my lesson today, citing a complicated case at work as his excuse. It had been a lot easier to concentrate without having him on the sidelines, picking holes in my riding and repeating Bruce's instructions whenever I came within earshot of him. I just hoped it wasn't a sign that he was still too angry with Bruce over the selections to talk to him. He'd refused to mention my coach's name in the house since the team announcement, and every time I brought him up, Dad's face clouded over.

I was tired of beating around the bush. "Was it because of my dad?"

Bruce looked startled by my direct approach, but he was never anything if not honest. "He can be, uh…"

153

"A pain in the butt," I finished for him.

Bruce cracked a small smile. "I was going to go with *liability*, but that's the gist of it, yeah."

"And Lily did so well at Nationals," I said, trying to give credit where it was due.

He shrugged. "She has a pair of very good ponies. We're going to have to hope she draws something very rideable overseas."

The look on his face didn't make it appear that he rated her chances, and my spirits lifted. I wondered if he'd voted for me, but I didn't want to ask.

"What happened to you down there?" Bruce asked, pushing his sunglasses back onto his head and scrutinising me. "You started out well, then fell apart in the last round."

I looked away from him. "I don't know. Had a bad night, I guess."

Bruce looked sceptical, but he accepted my answer. "Shame. You had a good lead going into that round. I heard you were looking at the Campbells' horse," he segued fluently as he started towards the arena gate.

I nudged Forbes into a walk and followed him. "I tried her, but it didn't work out."

"Good." Surprised, I glanced at Bruce as he opened the gate and swung it wide. "Too damn sensitive, that horse. It was never any use in Aussie either."

"That's not what they said."

"Course they didn't," Bruce scoffed. "Trying to sell it, weren't they?"

"Yeah, but…I saw videos." Well, I'd seen part of them. I refused to let myself think too much about that.

"I saw those videos too," Bruce replied. "And if that mare wasn't dosed to the eyeballs on calmers that day, I'll eat my hat."

Forbes's hooves crunched on the gravel as I rode him along the path towards the stables, thinking about what he'd just said.

"Poor Stacey," I said eventually.

Bruce grunted. "Poor Stacey nothing, I told her not to buy it and she wouldn't listen. That girl's either thick as two short planks, or just too bloody stubborn for her own good."

He stopped at his car, and hit the fob on the keyring that unlocked it. It bleeped, the lights flashing once, and Forbes jumped.

"Sorry mate." Bruce reached over and patted my pony's neck, crusty with dried sweat. "Same time next week?"

"Okay."

"Remember," he said, as he opened the front door of his car and leaned on it. "Variety is the spice of life." He pointed the key towards Forbes, who still had his ears fixed forward and was watching the vehicle with great suspicion in case it beeped at him again. "Take him out, let him see the world."

"I will. Thanks."

Bruce nodded, sliding into his car and pulling a face as he fired up the air conditioning. The sun was still baking down on us, and I could feel the skin on my arms starting to sizzle. As my coach drove away, Forbes relaxed, resting a hind leg and swishing his tail at the flies buzzing around us. I glanced over at the welcoming shade of the stables, then back up the driveway towards the road.

"Do you want to go on an adventure?"

I hadn't been lying when I'd told Bruce that I wasn't allowed to ride on the road, but there was no real reason for that rule other than my parents had decreed years ago that it wasn't safe. I had a vague memory of Pete having come off one of his ponies on the roadside years ago. He'd picked up a mild gravel rash and the pony had returned home unscathed, but it had frightened Mum and she'd refused to let him ride out on the roads again. Dad hadn't argued, except to tell Pete that he should've held onto the reins because he'd spent too much money on that pony for it to get hit by a car just because Pete couldn't hang onto it when he fell off. It wasn't a rule my parents had ever had to enforce, because I'd just taken it as read and never challenged it. But now I wondered. We lived on a quiet road with wide grass verges, and Forbes would benefit from another ten minutes or so of walking to stretch him out after his lesson. Besides, all the better to ride him out in strange territory when he was already tired. Much lower chance of being bucked off.

I clicked my tongue and rode Forbes forward and up the driveway. He baulked at first, spooking at the rose bushes and trying more than once to spin around and head for home, but I was insistent.

"We're expanding your horizons," I told the reluctant pony. "You'll thank me later, I promise."

Forbes was unconvinced until we reached the end of the driveway and turned left. Then his head came up and his ears pricked forward at the sight of the wide, flat grass verge laid out ahead of us. I kept the reins as loose as I could without relinquishing control, letting him swing his head to each side to check out the lay of the land. He took it in eagerly, watching the cows grazing in the neighbours' paddocks, flinching at the flapping washing line on the other side of the road, baulking at a yellow letterbox and going past it sideways with much eye-rolling, then stopping and snorting at the alpacas in the Hendersons' front paddock.

"Weird, huh?" I asked him, bracing myself for the possibility that he would spin on his haunches and bolt home, hopefully not throwing me off in the process. Forbes had led a quiet, sheltered life since he came to me, and his increasingly difficult behaviour was probably as much due to boredom as it was to a dislike of hard work.

After a couple of minutes of staring at the foreign creatures, Forbes crept forward, taking a few rushed steps before his courage failed him and he halted again, his eyes bugging out in alarm. The alpacas unhelpfully surged towards the fence, making Forbes panic, but I managed to keep him in place, and after a moment's staring at each other, they went back to grazing. I relaxed into the saddle, stroking Forbes with one hand and holding the reins in the other.

Cicadas whirred incessantly in the trees, punctuated occasionally by the warbles and croaks of tui. Beads of sweat trickled down my back as the sun baked down, its heat making the tarmac road shimmer ahead of us.

Forbes was still rooted in place, unwilling to go forward. He looked away from the alpacas for a moment, then swung his head back towards them, as though checking whether they were still there, and wouldn't just vanish if he wasn't looking directly at them. A car appeared in the distance, the sunlight glinting off the windshield as it flickered in and out of sight through the heat haze. Forbes spared it a quick glance, then returned his attention to the far more threatening gang of alpacas.

The car was moving fast, and as it came closer, I saw that it was a black Audi. My heart started beating faster as I wondered what Dad was going to say when he saw me out on the road, blatantly disobeying his instructions. I braced myself for a confrontation, but the car didn't slow down as it approached us, and I realised that it wasn't Dad after all. It was someone I didn't know, and they zoomed past us with their eyes fixed forward on the road ahead. Forbes flinched, but the car's safe passage apparently convinced him that it was safe to go past the alpacas without fear of certain death, although he insisted on doing so at a sideways trot.

As I shortened my reins and tried to get him to at least go in a straight line, I couldn't help smiling. We'd spend nearly an hour in the arena this afternoon trying to convince Forbes to trot slowly, but with cadence. He'd sworn black and blue that he just *couldn't* do any such thing, that it was physically *impossible* for a pony to even do that, and that I was being completely unreasonable.

Now, out on the side of the road and with nobody in sight, Forbes performed the most gorgeously springy, cadenced trot I'd ever had the privilege to sit on.

So Bruce told me today that Im first reserve for Ireland

I sent the message to Katy, then cracked another egg into the frying pan. Dad still wasn't home, and neither was Mum. I'd done the ponies, then sat in the house for half an hour with a rumbling stomach until I'd realised that there was nothing actually stopping me from making my own dinner. My whole life I'd grown up with dinner on the table at seven, but those rules didn't seem to apply to anyone else anymore, so why should they apply to me?

I hope you asked him why you werent in the team!!

I did, I typed back. **Dads fault. No surprise.**

I could almost see Katy's eye roll. **Bloody hell theyre thick. Like hes a pain (no offense) but surely they could keep him under control. Or you couldve just come with me and mum and left your dad at home! #betterplan**

I snorted as I added mushrooms to the pan. **Good luck with that he wouldn't have missed it for the world. well at least i know he didn't just buy me a place in the team... #silverlining ?**

Hah bet lilys parents did. Oh well first reserve is good though, now we just have to make sure lily doesn't make it and plenty of time for something to happen mwahaha ;)

I knew she was joking, but it still made my stomach twist to see that comment. *Too soon.*

Not funny, I wrote back quickly.

You know I didn't mean anything like THAT. Ugh well I can only hope that she'll break her arm or something. I'll pray for it every night lol. so hows buck doing?

Good! I typed back with one hand as I flipped my fried egg over in the pan. **New meds are working great and breathing is back to normal for now. Hes gonna have the winter off then we will reassess in the spring but I don't really care whether he comes back or not, i'm happy to retire him as long as hes comfortable and happy**

Buck's plaintive whinny reached me from the paddock outside as I sent the message. I'd put the other two into the barn to eat their feeds, and was hoping I could leave them in overnight, but Buck was feeling their absence, and the last thing I needed was to stress him out and have him start running around. I turned the gas hob off and went to the front door as Katy's reply buzzed in my hand.

That's so good! Yay buckles maybe he was just impatient to retire haha

I sent her a response as I stepped into my gumboots.

Idk about that he's having a meltdown bc the other two are in the barn tonight, so annoying he cant be stabled bc dust but wont let the others go in without freaking out arghh

The sun was setting behind me, bathing the barn in a pink glow. I walked around behind it to see Buck standing at the gate of his paddock, his head high and nostrils flared wide. He whinnied frantically when he noticed me, desperate to join his friends. I couldn't put him inside, but I couldn't leave him stressing like this either.

Fortunately the other two had finished their feeds, so I slipped a halter onto Forbes and led him out, opening Skip's stable as I passed it and letting him follow us back out to the paddock. He strode happily along behind us, stopping at the gate to Buck's small paddock to greet him. I debated letting him have a sleepover in his buddy's paddock, but I was worried that they'd start running around, and Buck still needed to be kept quiet.

I let Forbes go in the bigger paddock and came back for Skip, who was now grooming Buck's withers in the embrace of a long-lost friend.

I pulled my phone out of my pocket and took a photo, then sent it to Katy, followed by a tearful emoji. The ponies broke apart and looked at me, and I felt like a monster as I took hold of Skip's neck rug and reluctantly separated them.

"Sorry to break up the bromance of the century, but it's for your own good."

Buck tossed his head, not believing me, loudly voicing his protest as I led Skip into the other paddock. The two ponies had been fast friends from the day Skip had arrived, and they had always had a bit of separation anxiety, although they were both well-mannered enough for it not to show when I was riding. But the recent changes to Buck's routine and the stress of being sick was telling on him, and I just knew that if I let Skip stay with him for even one night, he would have a full-blown meltdown tomorrow. I didn't want him to be stressing himself out every time I took Skip out of his company, which would have to happen on a daily basis with Skip still in full work. And I had no clue what I was going to do with Buck when we went to Horse of the Year.

I cajoled a reluctant Skip back to his own paddock, where Forbes was grazing nonchalantly with his back to us. He didn't seem to give a hoot what anyone else was doing. My phone buzzed in my pocket as I walked back to see Buck, who was staring sadly at his friend, and I pulled it out to check the latest message from Katy.

Nawww poor lonely kid, maybe he needs a companion? You should get him a goat or something ;)

I glanced over my shoulder at Buck, wondering if that would work.

That's not the worst idea you've ever had …

"We need to talk."

I set down the magazine I'd been reading and looked at my father, looming in the doorway of my bedroom.

"Yes, we do. I think we should get Buck a companion, for when we go to shows or when the others go into the stables at night."

Dad blinked at me for a moment, confused by being thrown onto the back foot. But it didn't take him long to get back on track. "We can talk about that later." He came into my room and loomed over me, his arms folded.

"I think we should talk about it now. We need to do something before HOY, or he's going to be abandoned here on his own, and he'll have a meltdown. It's either that or we just scratch HOY altogether," I suggested, watching Dad's face carefully as I spoke.

"Don't be ridiculous. You're going to HOY." But there was a worried look in his eye that showed me he wasn't entirely convinced that he could make me do as he said anymore. "We'll bring the ponies home each night. Much safer than keeping them on the grounds in those rickety old stables."

"What about during the day? That's when his breathing's worst, and we're supposed to be having another heatwave. If he paces and screams from dawn to dusk…"

"All right, fine," Dad said, conceding defeat. "We'll sort something out with him. Now I wanted to talk about you, and what happened at that party."

I'd known this was coming, and tried to head him off at the pass. "I'm sorry."

"You said you wouldn't drink. You promised," Dad said, his voice becoming louder as he warmed to his subject. I wondered if he'd attract Mum's attention, then remembered that she was out with clients again. Undoubtedly that was part of what had made this seem like the ideal time to speak to me.

"I know. I'm sorry."

"Sorry isn't good enough," Dad warned me. "You're grounded. No more parties."

"Fine."

He seemed surprised by my easy capitulation. "That's okay with you, is it?"

I sighed. "Dad, in case you haven't noticed, I didn't exactly have the best time at Callie's. I'm not in a big hurry to go through all that again, so yeah, it's okay with me. Ban me from ever going to another party, I don't care."

He must have been bracing himself for a fight, because he didn't seem to know how to react to my compliance. "Well, good."

He uncrossed his arms and turned to leave, and I picked my magazine up again and looked at the diagrams of shoulder-in exercises, trying to memorise them for tomorrow's schooling session on Skip. From the corner of my eye, I saw my dad stop and turn back, one hand resting against the door frame.

"I'm sorry it didn't work out the way you'd hoped."

I met his eyes, unsure whether he was still talking about the party. I decided it didn't matter. "Me too."

Dad nodded, turned to leave again, then looked back another time. "And I'll see what I can do for Buck."

"Okay. Thanks."

He nodded once more, and left.

Catch the bus home today, I have meetings all afternoon and can't get away. Love Mum x

My mother has always been the only person I know who sends fully-punctuated text messages. I sent her an affirmative reply, then set my phone down on the table again and went back to studying. It was lunchtime and I was in the library, working on an upcoming assignment.

I hadn't been too surprised to discover that Callie and her friends had given me the cold shoulder from the moment I'd arrived at school on Monday morning. I was relieved to discover that I didn't really care, but I was back to being lonely. I told myself that it was better to have no friends than to have bad friends, but it didn't make it any easier to be so conspicuously alone.

I felt the table wobble as someone sat down opposite me, and glanced up to see Esther Blake. She tucked a strand of wavy auburn hair behind her ear and propped her chin in her hand, staring at me curiously.

"So what'd you do?"

"Excuse me?"

"To piss Callie off."

She raised an eyebrow at me curiously. At the end of last year, she'd been Callie's best friend. But something had happened over summer to shatter their friendship, and now Esther was left on the outside looking in. Like me.

"What'd *you* do?" I returned the question.

"You first."

I chewed the end of my pen, trying to work out how best to explain it without going into detail. "I just…couldn't be the person she wanted me to be."

Esther looked slightly surprised by my answer, then nodded slowly. "Couldn't, or wouldn't?"

I blinked, trying to decide. "Um…both, I guess."

"Good for you." Esther pulled her tablet out of its case and switched it on. "You're way too independent to be one of her minions anyway."

I liked the sound of that. "What about you?"

She just shrugged, her eyes on the tablet. "Same as you, basically. I was making too many of my own decisions, and had far too many of my own opinions for her liking. Callie's not happy unless she's got everyone wrapped around her little finger. I just got sick of it, that's all."

"Good for you," I said, echoing her comment from earlier.

Esther nodded and gave me a thumbs up. "Hey, you're in my Geography class, right? Have you started that earthquake assignment yet?"

I shook my head. "Nope. You?"

"Not yet. I'm just about to start." She lifted her head and looked

163

over at me consideringly. "Wanna join forces, work on it together?"

I thought for a moment, then nodded. "Sure. Why not?"

Esther grinned at me, showing a row of perfect white teeth. "Why not indeed?" She turned her attention back to her tablet, tapping away at the screen as she mumbled under her breath. "Why not indeed."

The bus dropped me off at the corner, leaving me to walk the half-kilometre home in the baking sun. It was one of those sweltering Hawke's Bay afternoons that made you just want to sit in the shade and eat icecream until dark. I knew I should've got up earlier and ridden Skip before school, but I hadn't had the energy. Now I was going to have to find that energy in the hottest part of the day, and I rued my decision with every step. Maybe I could wait until after dinner to ride – the daylight was sticking around until 9pm lately. But then I would have to get started on my homework right now, a prospect which didn't appeal at all after being shut up in school all day.

As I reached the front door, I heard the gravel crunch and looked around to see our truck driving in behind me. I wondered where Dad had been in the truck in the middle of the day. As far as I was aware it hadn't needed servicing, but he'd noticed the other week that the paintwork had been marked by Connor's little stunt, so maybe he'd taken it in for some touch-ups. I'd pleaded ignorance as to how it had happened, and I don't think he'd had any suspicions aroused.

I went inside the house, kicking off my shoes on my way to my room when Dad called me.

"There you are. Come out here for a minute."

"I'm just getting changed."

"It won't take long."

I sighed, taking a moment to pull on my paddock boots before following him back outside to where our truck was parked. He hit the button that lowered the hydraulic ramp as I reached his side.

"I thought about what you said," he told me. "So I made a few phone calls."

"Calls to who?"

"An old friend."

He handed me a lead rope as the ramp settled on the ground, and I stepped onto it, staring into the truck and wondering what on earth I was about to find. Four short legs were visible below the partition, and the glimpse of a flat, dark back.

"You got a…"

Before I could continue, I was interrupted by a deafening noise that reverberated around the inside of the truck, and I stared in astonishment at the little miniature donkey standing between the heavy partitions. She was a dark chocolate brown with a pale muzzle, and she looked at me, her long ears swaying as she moved her head.

"Well, hi," I said, reaching over to scratch her bristly mane. "I wasn't expecting you."

I unhooked the partition and pulled it back, revealing the donkey's shaggy coat and pot belly. She wouldn't win any beauty pageants, but she looked to be in fairly good health. I clipped up her lead rope and led her to the top of the ramp where she stopped and looked around, swivelling her huge ears like antennae. Skip and Forbes were in the furthest corner of their paddock, staring in horror at the donkey and snorting loudly at each other, clearly not impressed with the newest addition to the family.

"What d'you think of her?"

I looked at my father with a smile. "She's super cute," I admitted. "Though I don't know what Buck's going to think of her. What's her name?"

"Emily." Dad pulled a face, and I laughed. His sister's name was Emily, and she'd definitely be offended to hear that we had a donkey named after her, even unintentionally.

"That's perfect," I told him with a grin as I started forward down the ramp. Emily took two more steps then brayed again, and this time, to my astonishment, I heard Buck whinny back.

I looked at Dad curiously, but he was poker-faced as I led the little donkey around the side of the stables towards Buck's paddock. Forbes was prancing around in the far corner of the paddock and snorting like a bull, while Skip stood stock still, his eyes firmly fixed on the wee donkey, ready to bolt away at any moment. But Buck was waiting by the gate to his paddock with his ears pricked, ready to meet his new friend.

I looked at Dad in astonishment as I walked Emily right up to the gate, and Buck leaned over and they sniffed each other's muzzles. The greeting was short-lived, as Emily decided that it was more important to munch on the grass at her feet than to meet her new companion. Buck leaned harder on the gate and nickered to her, and I decided it was probably safe to introduce them.

"I knew you were lonely," I told Buck, waving him out of the way of the gate as I unlatched it and led Emily through. "But I didn't think you were *this* desperate to have a buddy."

Dad shut the gate behind me as I removed Emily's halter. She stood politely until her head was freed, then turned and wandered off across the paddock, looking around at her new accommodation as Buck followed her like a lovesick puppy.

"It's like they're already friends," I exclaimed in amazement, then saw the look on my father's face as he grinned at me.

"They are," he confirmed, leaning on the gate next to me and watching them with satisfaction. "At least, they were. I got to thinking about what you'd said, so I rang around his former owners to see if he'd had a companion animal before, and Laura said she'd kept him with a miniature donkey." He waved a hand towards Emily, who was walking slowly around the perimeter of the paddock, her pale muzzle brushing the tips of the dry grass with Buck still in steady pursuit. "Turned out that she still had Emily on the farm, just

166

standing around getting fat, so she said we're welcome to have her for as long as we want."

I grinned at him. "I would never have thought of that. Well done, Dad. And on Buck's behalf, thank you."

I could feel the warmth bubbling inside me at the sight of my pony finally looking happy again.

Dad squeezed my shoulder, then stepped back. "You're both welcome. I'll leave you to clean the truck out. For a small donkey, she sure made one helluva mess."

That evening, after my homework was finished, I went out to the paddock to check on Buck. I'd stabled the other two ponies earlier, and although Buck had whinnied to Skip when I put him inside, I hadn't heard a peep out of him since. But I wanted to make sure that all was well.

It was almost dark, and I followed the track lighting that led to the barn. The doors were left open to let the air flow through, and I poked my head in and checked on the other two ponies. Forbes was still pulling at his net of freshly steamed hay, and Skip was dozing in the corner of his box. I left them to it, and made my way quietly around to the paddock behind the barn.

It took me a moment to pick out Buck's shape out of the darkness. He was standing in the middle of his paddock, and swivelled his head to look at me as I approached the gate. Emily was lying at his feet, her short legs tucked underneath her, her mealy muzzle resting on the ground as she slept.

Buck whiffled his nostrils at me welcomingly, then dipped his nose towards Emily, as though thanking me for bringing her back. I smiled at him, staying at the gate so I didn't disturb the little donkey's slumber.

"You're welcome," I whispered to Buck. "I'm just glad you're okay now."

And I left him to doze under the stars with his little friend as I walked back up to the house to finish my homework.

♥

Don't miss the next books in the Pony Jumpers series!

Pony Jumpers #8
EIGHT AWAY

Pony of the Year is approaching fast, and everyone in Tess's family is determined to see her compete in the prestigious event – everyone, that is, except Tess herself. She has never liked riding the exuberant show jumper Misty Magic, and a crashing fall during training leaves Tess bruised, battered…and terrified of getting back into the saddle.

While her sister Hayley's future hangs in the balance as she prepares to undergo invasive surgery to try and save her life, Tess is blindsided by the revelation that the one person she thought she could count on may have been lying to her all along.

Can Tess find a way to conquer her fears once and for all, or will she let her sister down when it matters the most?

♥

Pony Jumpers Special Edition #1
JONTY

Jonty Fisher hasn't grown up with horses. Hasn't grown up with much of anything, tell you the truth, except a love for being outdoors and a restless energy he can't quite contain. The unexpected arrival of a bedraggled black pony on his eleventh birthday marks the beginning of a new direction in his life, setting him on a path that will determine what he can make of his future.

But as Jonty's desire to prove himself builds, the school of hard knocks never fails to keep pushing him back down, and it will take a lot of courage, resilience and heart for him to find a way to follow his dreams.

Still, if life was meant to be easy, everyone would do it…

ACKNOWLEDGEMENTS

Many thanks to Sheila Ramsay, Rachel Fouhy and Carissa McCall for their assistance and support during the writing of this novel, answering my endless questions about the details of strangles, respiratory illness and its treatment, both immediate and long-term. Their time and assistance was very much appreciated. I hope that I have the details correct – and remember, if in doubt, to always consult your veterinarian, as prevention is infinitely better than cure.

For more about me and the books I have written, you can visit my website at **nzponywriter.com**, where you can sign up for my mailing list to get new release information, updates and enter giveaways. You can also find me on Facebook as **Kate Lattey - Author** and on Instagram at **@kate_lattey**.

Finally, if you enjoyed reading this book, please consider leaving a review on Amazon or Goodreads to encourage others to give it a try.

ABOUT THE AUTHOR

Kate Lattey lives in Waikanae, New Zealand and started riding at the age of 10. She was lucky enough to have ponies of her own during her teenage years, and competed regularly in show jumping, eventing and mounted games before finishing college and heading to university, graduating with a Bachelor of Arts in English & Media Studies.

In the years since, she has never been far from horses, and has worked in various jobs including as a livery yard groom in England, a trekking guide in Ireland, a riding school manager in New Zealand, and a summer camp counselor in the USA. It was during her time there that Kate started writing short stories about the camp's horses, which were a huge hit with the campers, and inspired Kate to continue pursuing her passion for writing.

Kate currently owns a Welsh Cob x Thoroughbred gelding named JJ, and competes in show jumping and show hunter competitions, as well as coaching at Pony Club and judging at local events.

She has been reading and writing pony stories ever since she can remember, and has many more yet to come! If you enjoyed this book, check out the rest of the series and her other novels on Amazon, and visit nzponywriter.com to sign up for her mailing list and get information about new and upcoming releases.

DARE TO DREAM

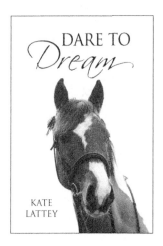

Saying goodbye to the horses they love has become a way of life for Marley and her sisters, who train and sell show jumpers to make their living. Marley has grand ambitions to jump in Pony of the Year, but every good pony she's ever had has been sold out from under her to pay the bills.

Then a half-wild pinto pony comes into her life, and Marley finds that this most unlikely of champions could be the superstar she has always dreamed of. As Marley and Cruise rise quickly to the top of their sport, it seems as though her dream might come true after all.

But her family is struggling to make ends meet, and as the countdown to Pony of the Year begins, Marley is forced to face the possibility of losing the pony she has come to love more than anything else in the world.

Can Marley save the farm she loves, without sacrificing the pony she can't live without?

DREAM ON

"Nobody has ever tried to understand this pony.
Nobody has ever been on her side. Until now.
She needs you to fight for her, Marley. She needs you to love her."

Borderline Majestic was imported from the other side of the world to bring her new owners fame and glory, but she is almost impossible to handle and ride. When the pony lands her rider in intensive care, it is up to Marley to prove that the talented mare is not dangerous - just deeply misunderstood.

Can Marley dare to fall in love again to save Majestic's life?

This much-anticipated sequel to *Dare to Dream* was a Top 20 Kindle Book Awards Semi-Finalist in 2015.

Clearwater Bay #1
FLYING CHANGES

When Jay moves from her home in England to live with her estranged father in rural New Zealand, it is only his promise of a pony of her own that convinces her to leave her old life behind and start over in a new country.

Change doesn't come easily at first, and Jay makes as many enemies as she does friends before she finds the perfect pony, who seems destined to make her dreams of show jumping success come true.

But she soon discovers that training her own pony is not as easy as she thought it would be, and her dream pony is becoming increasingly unmanageable and difficult to ride.

Can Jay pull it all together, or has she made the biggest mistake of her life?

Clearwater Bay #2
AGAINST THE CLOCK

It's a new season and a new start for Jay and her wilful pony Finn, but their best laid plans are quickly plagued by injuries, arguments and rails that just won't stay in their cups. And when her father introduces her to his new girlfriend, Jay can't help wondering if her life will ever run according to plan.

While her friends battle with their own families and Jay struggles to define hers, it is only her determination to bring out the best in her pony that keeps her going. But after overhearing a top rider say that Finn's potential is being hampered by her incompetent rider, Jay is besieged by doubts in her own ability…and begins to wonder whether Finn would be better off without her.

Can Jay bear to give up on her dreams, even if it's for her pony's sake?

Also by Kate Lattey

PONY JUMPERS

DARE TO DREAM

CLEARWATER BAY

For more information, visit nzponywriter.com

Email nzponywriter@gmail.com and sign up to my mailing list
for exclusive previews, new releases, giveaways and more!

Printed in Great Britain
by Amazon

87011039R00102